ACCIDENT

Books by Nicholas Mosley

Spaces of the Dark
The Rainbearers
Corruption
Meeting Place
Accident
Impossible Object
Natalie Natalia
The Catastrophe Practice Series:
   Hopeful Monsters
   Imago Bird
   Serpent
   Judith
   Catastrophe Practice

NONFICTION

African Switchback
The Life of Raymond Raynes
Experience and Religion
The Assassination of Trotsky
Julian Grenfell
Rules of the Game/Beyond the Pale:
   Memoirs of Sir Oswald Mosley and Family

Nicholas Mosley

ACCIDENT

With an afterword by
Steven Weisenburger

Dalkey Archive Press

Library of Congress Catalogue Number: 85-072479
ISBN: 0-916583-11-2

Partially funded by a grant from The Illinois Arts Council.

Dalkey Archive Press
1817 North 79th Avenue
Elmwood Park, IL 60635 USA

Printed on permanent/durable acid-free paper and bound in the United States of America.

I

1.

TREES at night are like an army marching. I came across the car on its side across the road. It stretched from bank to bank like the stump of a tree uprooted.

I had been coming down the road with my torch making a circle on the gravel. The underneath of the car was towards me mottled with drops of earth like rain. I climbed on the side of the car. My torch reappeared beneath me moving in glass at different levels. There was a fast ticking like a clock with the pendulum gone. I registered this—the petrol pump. I opened the front door upwards, lying on my back and pushing with a hand and foot. I put my torch in my mouth. My breath made a snoring sound. The door crashed back against the body of the car and my torch swung downwards. I thought I had lost all my teeth.

I said—"William?"

Inside there was the ignition key. I turned it and the ticking stopped. There were bodies—piled and untouchable.

Rolling to my front and resting my torch on the edge of the door making lights inside like diamonds I reached down and touched cloth, soft, that thing of bones, untouchable.

I said—"Anna?"

Anna groaned.

I began pulling at her. I did not know if you did this. The bones in the white skin sharp as razors. I thought—Somebody help me.

The indecency of the dead.

Anna screamed.

I said "Anna, where is it?"

She began pushing against something below her, climbing with her shoes on its face. I thought—They always do this.

I said "Are you all right?"

She reared up out of the car with her head and shoulders, the clouds and the white moon moving above her. She pushed her hair back. There was the smell of petrol. And another smell, sickening.

I shouted "You're standing on him!"

She came out of the car like a dancer, myself lifting her, my hands on her thighs. I said "Am I hurting you?" We turned in the air and moved towards the trees and the dark bank. I lowered her and my head went on to the ground. There was something on my hair, my hands. I made a circle of finger and thumb and drew it up each finger. It had no colour, smell.

Climbing on to the car again and looking down I saw William with his face to the ground among the glass splinters. I tried to get into the back seat but the front door had fallen back so I had to lower myself through the front with my legs sideways not to stand on him. I knelt on the broken glass, my hand out, the blood tasting clean. The car like a diving bell.

I said—"William?"

I knew he was dead. I felt his wrist, shoulder. How one does know this. I put my head against his neck and listened.

Anna appeared above me, her huge body at the window. She leaned right into the car with her arms hanging down.

I pushed at her.

One of her hands reached a handbag by William's feet. She helped me raise her, one hand on the steering wheel. The steering wheel was in the top half of the car.

I began walking up the road towards the telephone.

Anna was sitting on the bank. She had opened her bag and was doing something to her face with a handkerchief.

I had emerged from the car head and shoulders. The trees and the night sky. The steering wheel was at my waist. When I had leaned down, and had first touched Anna, I had had one hand on the steering wheel.

I began walking up the road towards the telephone. Somewhere I had smelled whisky. In the broken glass at the bottom, on the bank where I had lowered Anna. Anna had been on top of William. I stood and watched her. She was wiping her mouth.

I said "Can you walk?"

She did not look at me. She was wearing an evening dress, white, with a skirt that bulged up in a hoop. The grass and the dark bank with dampness on it.

I said "I'm going to telephone."

I walked up the lane towards my house. Three minutes to the back gate and the grey posts rotting. In the hall there were broken toys and a bicycle. The dog came towards me, shivering. I said into the telephone "There's an accident in Copper Lane, could you come quickly?"

I sat by the telephone. Night, objects, expectant. I should be running. Time catching up with me.

I was going out of the house again when Anna was there

7

on the doorstep, an apparition. She was holding her bag in front of her: her head in profile: a ruined housemaid. The trees in the sky like dead banners. I said "Anna, are you all right?" I felt her arms, shoulders. The smell of whisky again. I said "Come in." I led her through to the sitting room and turned on an electric fire. She sat in a chair. She did not do anything.

Her hair fair and her flat face puffy. Her dress with her body coming out of it like a bathing dress. Toes turned inwards. I thought—I should get a blanket. There was blue wall-paper and a yellow rug and black curtains with a gold pelmet. The police and the ambulance would be coming. Cranes and searchlights. I put my hand on Anna's head. The skull was small, fragile. I said "Were you driving?" Her head was by my thighs. I said "Don't worry, Anna." The dead time. Running down of the world. Two o'clock in the morning.

The policeman was our village policeman. He had a tapering head that seemed to have fitted itself to his helmet like a nut. He held his helmet under his arm. He said— "Codrington, Mr. William Codrington."

I said "That's right."

I was sitting in the chair that Anna had been sitting in.

He said "Do you know what he might have been doing?"

I said "Won't you sit down?"

The policeman put his helmet on the floor.

He said "He might have been coming to see you?"

I said "I'm the only house for some distance up the lane."

"But you did know him?"

"He was my pupil."

8

"At the university?"

"Yes."

He had his notebook, folded over backwards, and a yellow pencil.

"Would he have a reason to come and see you?"

I said "He'd been at this party." I felt I was ill. I put a hand to my forehead. I could make myself ill. I said—"A party at college, he must have come from there."

The policeman looked at me. A yellow face. Round. The eyes not seeing anything.

I said "Does it matter?" I added "Now?"

The policeman said "You needn't say anything if you don't want to."

I said "I think he was in some trouble. He wanted to see me."

The policeman said "Trouble."

I said "They come to us for all sorts of things. Perhaps I shouldn't say this."

The policeman turned back a page of his notebook. A board creaked upstairs. I thought—I can say it is my wife, my children.

He said "You came across the car about one forty-five?"

"Yes, I heard it. At least I thought I did."

"And you went down the lane."

"Yes."

"And you found the car on its side. You thought Mr. Codrington was already dead. You did not move him. You came back and rang the police."

I did not think he would have remembered all this. There had been the police, a car, and an ambulance. I had gone back when I had left Anna. I had talked to them. I had said—

9

I didn't move him. They had lifted him from the car, a man in a mackintosh, the policeman, and a man in a white coat. William was wearing a white tie. The ambulance had a blue light. The men had stood with their backs to me.

I had left Anna in the chair in the sitting room.

The policeman said "Is that correct?"

I said "Yes." I thought—I should be getting him out of the house. Doing something.

The policeman closed his book. He said "We have to ask these questions."

I said "He was my friend." The policeman had half stood up. Now he sat down again.

I could not think what else I might have said. They had lifted William into the ambulance. There had been a brown blanket at his head and feet. A crane with a hook on the front of the car. The policeman had said—May I use your telephone? When we got back to the house Anna was not there. I had left her in the chair in which I was now sitting.

The policeman said "It was his car?"

I said "Yes."

I did not know where Anna had gone. I had come into the sitting room in front of the policeman. I had left him by the telephone. I had intended to say—Go, Anna, if you want to. But Anna had gone.

The policeman said "I think the rest can wait."

I stood up. We went into the hall. Anna had had a bag. She had not had a bag in the sitting room. It was an evening bag, long, made of black velvet.

The policeman said "I'll call you in the morning."

I said "Please do."

He looked at me. I thought—The bag is not in the hall.
I said "They all drive too fast."
He said "They do."
I closed the door behind him. I stood with my back to it.
I was pretending to keep something out. Surrounded. Till
morning.

I moved through the house like someone bankrupt before
the bailiffs arrive; through the dining room, kitchen, this
is where Anna and Charlie had once sat: he like a satyr
taking a bite out of her neck, she a white Rubens with fruit
in her hair. To the back yard where Anna might be hiding
(I imagined) standing in the dark among the coal and dustbins with the trees and black clouds moving. What we have
asked for; choice, freedom. I went back into the house and
listened. There was the sound of cats in a cavern, with the
rocks of walls dripping. I went up the stairs. Here Anna
had once appeared with her hair dark and different so I
had not recognised her. In those days we had lived so much
in our minds, like policemen. I went on the landing to the
spare room which had a four-poster bed and grey curtains
and a square armchair. Anna was lying on the bed with
shoes off and her skirt in the air, no stockings. Fallen in
some ballet on a tomb. She had stayed here once before
when she had come with William. Had borrowed a black
nightdress which I had afterwards kept in a drawer. Her legs
went up into the top of her skirt and disappeared there.
Thick, rather puffy face. Boyish, like a cherub. Austrians
had these faces; their eyes far apart. Her mother had been
English. Anna's mouth was open as if she had been hit.
Fair hairs near the edge of it.

Her bag was on the dressing table. Two screwed-up paper handkerchiefs beside it.

I felt tears coming to my eyes. Tried to encourage them. We had lived so much in our minds, dry and waiting.

Terrified.

I went down to the hall again, to the telephone. I gave a number and told the exchange to go on ringing. There was the night. Silence. The dead time. Objects coming alive and waiting.

I said "Charlie? Listen—"

II

2.

MY name is Stephen Jervis. I am a fellow of St. Mark's College, Oxford. I teach philosophy.

I have a room in college that looks out over the green lawns of a quadrangle. On the grass there is a white goat tethered. The peg to which the goat is tethered is moved from time to time, which makes overlapping circles like ancient earthworks seen from an aeroplane.

I have about eighteen pupils who each come to me for an hour each week. These tutorials are my main work, though I sometimes lecture and have a minor job in college administration.

When my pupils come to me they cross the quadrangle where the goat is tied and they climb uncarpeted stairs making a noise like a house with no furniture. My room is long and low with a central beam supported by oak pillars. There are books along one long wall and opposite it high windows with a deep ledge in front. I stand with my elbows on this ledge and look out on the goat, the circled lawn.

We sometimes have pupils sent to us from the women's colleges. These are on some special course or unable to be dealt with by their own colleges. One of my pupils at the beginning of the summer term was Anna von Graz und Leoben.

Particulars of our pupils come to us at the beginning of term on a list. Anna had been one year at a German university; had come to Oxford to read politics, philosophy and economics. She had taken her entrance exam in languages. She was due for her term reading philosophy.

At the beginning of each term there is a starting-up of machinery; people moving along stone paths again in and out of shadows. As I lean on the window-ledge of my room I see this image of myself—a man in a gown with rather long hair flowing, caught against the wall of a crumbling building.

The first time I saw Anna she squatted down by the goat to talk to it. The shadow of the rope made a thick line on the grass. A big blonde girl in a tartan skirt. The goat was tufted.

I hardly heard her come up the stairs. She must have crept like a mother in a fairy story.

I can do my introductory talk about philosophy without much thinking about it. Philosophy is a work, a process of enquiry: it's not an empirical science leading to laws and conclusions nor a formal deduction like mathematics. Its business is to discover and clarify the categories by which we think, and thus to allow the construction of more adequate terms and models. It does not find specific answers to specific questions, but rather deals with questions to which there are no specific answers. There is a lot of nonsense talked about philosophy nowadays; people say it is no longer a guide to everyday experience. This criticism is superficial. There is no more useful work than to illuminate old obscurities and contradictions, and by understanding them prevent more pathological confusions. For the rest— for what has to grow—this has to be found by the whole of life, and not particularly by intellectual discipline.

My pupils sit, and look at their notebooks, and sometimes write something down with their pencils. I wonder what they are thinking.

I sometimes ask—"Why do you want to do philosophy?"

What I am saying is only half true. There is a part of me which knows that philosophy is more negative, a way of limiting personality. But so is all routine. What do we do about this—in any form—we do not know.

I said—"Have you done any of this before?"

Anna said she had done some in Germany, where she believed it was different.

I said "What have you read?"

She said Nietzsche, Heidegger.

I said Yes, it was different.

She had only a faint foreign accent. A wide face, eyes set far apart. There are people you don't like to look at. You feel you know.

Some of my pupils I recognise to have the same talent as myself—a sort of alertness, an irony about them. With these people I can work; we learn together. With others we cover the ground but leave no mark. There is a sort of distrust about them. I catch them looking at me as if they do not hear, or as if I am saying something different from what I imagine. It is something to do with being still young; sleeping. But with these I sometimes feel an interest quite apart from what I am teaching.

I said "We'll be doing the seventeenth and eighteenth centuries, metaphysics, Descartes and Locke and so on. See how you manage. I'll give you some reading. It's mainly a question of seeing what the problem is."

She said "What is the problem?"

I said "That's what you've got to find out."

She had those slightly protuberant eyes of aristocrats. Inbred, a softness about them; to be sucked in and swallowed. She wore a white blouse to the waist. Sunburnt.

I said "Read the *Discourse on Method*. See what you think. Write me an essay on—"

I went to the ledge in front of the window, leaned on it, frowned, took out my pipe. I go through these rituals as part of the timing, the filling-in of areas. I looked for matches, pressed my pipe, blew through it. The hard wood under my elbow. The relationship between teacher and pupil being a sort of parade, marching backwards and forwards in column. Then a halt and a sudden turning in line.

I said "Write me an essay on just what the problem is."

I ticked off some lectures on a list. I gave her the names of books and she wrote them down. I went to my chair and sat with my body almost horizontal. Teaching is a burden, one person imparting something to another. Sometimes this happens directly like a gift. This is no good: talking to oneself.

Anna had fair hair. Clearly defined lips. No lipstick.

Between puffs on my pipe I spoke hesitantly. I frowned and held the stem like a gun against my forehead. Teaching has to be thrown over like something on the floor. Then people can either pick it up or not, as they want to.

I said "Are you a Catholic?"

She said "Yes."

I remembered Charlie saying—Never trust a girl who's a Catholic.

I said "Have you read Catholic philosophy?"

She said "No."

I said "It's a difficult essay I've set you, in a way it's the last question."

At the beginning of term that year, May, it was already hot. The sun came through the windows on to areas of skin, of furniture. Feeling in concentrated areas with the heat moving across them.

I said "You've settled in all right?"

She said "It's my second term."

I said "Of course. You're at St. Margaret's?"

I wondered if I should ask about her life. She sat with her knees close together; surprisingly thin legs. But you go at this thing backwards: do the opposite of what you want. I knew all this. I leaned forwards with my hands on the arms of the chair. She got up. Carrying books, a notebook, a big brown bag with a strap.

When she had gone, I stood with my arms on the ledge of the window and looked out on to the lawn. I thought— You never know a person; only what you put into them, their effects. A platitude. The shadow from the roof of the building made a line with two angles at the gutter and the ground. Once I had wanted to be an architect. Fitting things in: filling spaces.

I was forty that year. The generation of my pupils had something blank about them: they were an appearance, clothes, shape, colour, skin. As if something had been exorcised in them. Cautious. Listening. Except the bright characters in funny trousers still having photographs taken of themselves like a cricket eleven in the 1880's.

Or perhaps it was myself.

In this room—oak pillars, bookshelves, papers, electric fire—I am very much on my own. I am an instrument, a working thing. The consolations of work are that you come from it tired at the end of a long day. A robot, with men working inside you. They pull levers; switch. You watch and move. At the end you have something to look forward to. You go home. To rest. The mechanism sleeps. The men open doors, windows. Look out into the air.

3.

I live a few miles outside Oxford in a house that was once a farmhouse but had a new front stuck on to it in the nineteenth century and is now called Palling Manor.

In front of it is a hollow with the old village of church, pub, whitewashed cottages and one shop with an enamel advertisement for cigarettes. There are council houses on the hill opposite. At the back is open country with a narrow lane to the main road to Oxford. This lane comes close to the house and then curves away to avoid the hollow. There is a footpath from the front of the house to the village.

Driving home from Oxford along a dual carriageway there is some point on the road at which I move away from the person which I am in college and go into the person I am at home.

On either side of the front door of my house is a heraldic lion in stone. The hall is an unused room that has become a repository for garden tools and toys. The rooms at the front of the house lead into one another with a door into the garden at each end so that in cold weather they are like a wind tunnel. You go through the dining room like a passage into the sitting room at the back which is the only room on the ground floor like a room, with a good fireplace and bow-window. Here my wife and children sit. There is a moment when I feel like a stranger, when I am going through the dining room like a passage towards the sitting room.

My wife sits in a chair half turned to catch the light. She is sewing, some cotton or needle in her mouth, giving her a look as if she were facing into a gale. Around us are the windfalls of our common life—books, paintboxes, papers in strips, scissors, children's magazines, the two children themselves, their heads close together, kneeling. A domestic interior. Before I speak someone has spoken first—a question or protest, inwards, between the three. They have a closed circuit, the three of them, the children grown upwards from the roots of her. My son Alexander, aged seven, has huge gentle eyes. Looking at him you see all children, archetypal. My daughter Clarissa, three, is Freudian. She holds her arms out and runs towards her mother. From over her mother's shoulder she flashes black eyes at me.

I say "She loves her dad."

My wife says "She hasn't eaten anything today."

On the largest armchair there is a fire engine and a game of ludo. The father comes home and wants to be entertained. The mother is bored and wants to be comforted. We know all this.

I say "How much has she eaten?"

My wife says "Some milk pudding at lunch."

I say "Then that's marvellous."

We act this out. We have been married nine years. We still need time; it is difficult coming home. Marriages break

19

because people don't wait enough. You have to carry this.

My wife says "Don't be cross."

I say "I'm not cross."

My wife is pregnant again. I mean, she was pregnant at the time about which I am writing. I write in the present because there seems something timeless about this scene— two people loving and irritated with one another. In a room, with time outside. If you carry it the thing works. If you don't, it doesn't.

My daughter Clarissa runs across the room and bangs into my leg, buries her face there, wraps her arms around me. I lean down and hold her beneath thin shoulders. She lifts her legs and hangs on to me like a tree. I say "My love, my ladybird." My son Alexander follows with his huge eyes hurting. I put out a hand and ruffle his short hair. I say "My boyo, what did you do at school today?" He leans on me, face like roses. I try to put an arm round both, the children I love, the all of life to me. Alexander carries a toy gun with which he pokes Clarissa. Clarissa screams. I say "Come on, we'll read a story!" Clarissa rubs her mouth against my trousers. I say to Alexander "Find that book about the elephant." I make a face with my cheeks blown out. Alexander goes off as if on a ship in a rough sea, lurching and hanging on to the furniture. I hobble to a chair with Clarissa still clinging to my leg. I take off the fire engine and the ludo. I sit and lift Clarissa on to my lap.

Now that I am the person I am at home, this room with yellow carpet, black curtains, heavy gold pelmet—I look round as if to recognise this. The only room in our house which is like a room, rather rich, where that white-haired man with an eye patch might stand by a bottle of sherry.

My wife Rosalind has short fair hair in a fringe then falling to the level of her chin. She has the sort of face that could at almost any age play St. Joan beautifully—a marvellous face with no make-up and sometimes spiritually marvellous—a depth of feminine knowledge that tears the heart out nowadays because it is so rare.

Alexander says "I can't find the book."

I say "Go on looking for it."

Rosalind says "Have you got anyone new this term?"

Clarissa lies in my arms with her gold hair spread out. Grass in a green field and love on its back.

I say "I've got a princess, or a countess, or something."

Rosalind groans.

I tickle Clarissa and make a noise like a bath running out.

Alexander says "Mummy I can't find the book."

Rosalind says "Alexander you are helpless."

She puts down her sewing, cotton, needle in her mouth; steps over the strips of paper and paintbox; Alexander watching like someone wounded.

I say "She's a bogus countess: German or Austrian, I think."

Rosalind says "Yum yum."

I don't know how other married couples talk to each other. Charlie and Laura, who are the other married couple we know best, say that on their own they never talk at all.

I bounce Clarissa on my knee. I sing "Baby baby bunting, daddy goes a-hunting."

Rosalind says "You are disgusting."

I say "She's not my type."

A cloud has come across Clarissa. She begins to sing in her small high voice "Daddy not go hunting!"

I put my cheek down on to her soft gold head. I rock her to and fro and say "No, my lovely, daddy not go hunting."

Rosalind is holding Alexander. She says "I didn't mean it, my beautiful monster boy."

From where I hold my head I look down along Clarissa's black tights like a ballet dancer towards her small waving shoe. I wonder if I have done what I wanted to do with Anna. I would see her every week for eight weeks.

Rosalind is leaning above me. She says "Mama wants a little love too."

I stroke her cheek and say "Now we are almost human again."

Her face coming down, dreaming, in close-up.

She says "I don't know what you mean."

I say "You're always so awful when I get home."

She says "You are."

The soft lines at her mouth, her eyes. I put my arm around her. Her skirt. I say "You know all this."

She says "I'm a pregnant lady."

I hold her.

Alexander shouts "I've found it!"

Everyone happy again. The children sit on each knee. The book, a dull one, is about an elephant chased in a motor boat. The drawings are like rude postcards. The minds of children work in myths which we have forgotten. Clarissa picks her nose. Alexander leans. Rosalind has gone back to her sewing. I remember I have some work to do. I have left it in the car. I wonder if there will be anything on television this evening.

4.

William Codrington was another pupil of mine. He was the younger son of a family whose house the public pay two-and-six to go round in the summer. He was a quiet, ill-at-ease boy with his head on one side and a smile that made his whole face melt like butter. He had this dissolution about him that aristocrats have: a sort of crafty toughness, mostly defeated.

William would come up my stairs in college two at a time, a slow tread like a climber with rucksack. A pause before he knocked. Then he put his head round.

"Come in, come in."

"You're not busy?"

He sometimes seemed to be crippled, his legs in splints.

"What do you want?"

"I want to ask about one of your pupils."

He used his charm like an old fencer conserving energy.

"Sit down, sit down, what do you want to know about her?"

"Oh I suppose everyone wants to know about her."

"Absolutely no one, I've been sitting here day after day just waiting for someone to come in and ask about her."

William and I knew each other quite well. We used to talk like this, showing off, perhaps learning something from each other. I was rather fascinated by aristocrats at this time: was not ashamed of this. But I sometimes found myself almost flirting with William, which I afterwards hated.

"Who, what, is she?"

"We are talking of the same person?"

"Of course."

"Her family?"

"Yes."

I said—"I don't know about her family. What about yours, for God's sake?"

I was encouraging William to get away from his family, feeling this was the only hope for him like younger sons who go to Australia.

"I thought a good tutor should be interested in his pupils' private lives."

This conversation took place, I think, about the second week of term. I had been sitting in my room reading essays. I kept my pupils' essays after they had read them to me at tutorials and went through them on my own.

I said "Because she's a princess or countess or something?" I remembered saying something like this before.

William said "She's very attractive."

"So everyone's after her?"

I was trying to find Anna's notebook in the pile. People seem attractive by being thought so by others. A platitude. Men banding together: puffing their feathers out and drawling.

I said "She's obviously clever. Read modern German and all that balls."

William said "Is German philosophy all balls?"

I shouted "Of course not!"

I found Anna's notebook and held it open. I read rapidly in a sing-song voice—" 'Descartes in his search for an absolute certainty had come across the proposition I think therefore I am—of which he thought he could be sure beyond reasonable doubt, so from this one proposition he attempted to create a synthetic system, but from his ultimate premise he produced conclusions which were not warranted.' "

I said "Yes, yes."

William said "That's all right?"

I said "You're fond of her?"

William said "What a word!"

I said "She's probably better than most of your girls."

I thought—How awful. William sat with his queer soft face. I felt annoyed. I could not remember being in love. That pain. Defencelessness. I thought—We wish their destruction.

William said "I've only met her once or twice. Of course it's ridiculous."

I jumped to my feet. "Why ridiculous?"

"I don't know what she thinks of me."

I shouted "What does that matter?"

William said nothing.

I said "Try it, for God's sake. Have you decided what you're going to do when you leave?"

William said "No."

"Still agriculture?"

William said "What ought I to do?"

I said "You'll get a good degree. Second class. There are a lot of jobs in the world."

William looked hurt. I thought—They want to be defeated.

William said "I might go to Italy for a bit."

I thought—A girl like Anna would eat him.

After William had gone I went out into the sun. There was time for a walk before lunch. I was restless that summer; always wanting to move, from A to B, between appointments. The lilac was out; cherry blossom had fallen and blown away like confetti. I wondered why I was not more sensible with William. Something unconscious: almost homosexual. We analyse ourselves too much; we know all this. I was fond of William: by joking I could touch him. There were some dons who only cared about their work and nothing about their pupils: these touched no one. All caring was risky: you exposed yourself. It was better to be like this than the other. I was justifying myself. With the sun out. In the summer.

5.

The fellows of St. Mark's College meet at lunch. We come from different directions through stone vaults and cream painted corridors and emerge in a first floor room that once was a library. There are book-cases covered with wire around three walls and a long table with a cloth on in the middle. I do not know why we eat here; it is a custom the origins of which are forgotten. We have each meal of the day in a different room; to keep ourselves moving.

We queue at a cold buffet by the sideboard: then walk to a group down the long table.

What makes us choose our group—carrying cold pork, salad, baked potato—is something to do with intrigue, or rivalries, with which we are obsessed. I chose a group with

Hedge, a mathematician, a man with such a low bridge to his nose that the lenses of his spectacles were joined at the bottom: Arthurson, ancient languages, with a stiff collar against his adam's apple like a bacon slicer: and Tommy Parker, historian, wearing Italian-style trousers and a black polo-neck sweater. Tommy Parker had recently been appearing on television, which made us both envy and fear him, like a primitive king or witch-doctor.

Tommy Parker had propped *Sporting World* against a water jug. He said "I see Max de Woppa spent three minutes in the sin bin."

Arthurson said "I thought bin referred to a lunatic asylum."

I said "That's the laughing academy."

I thought that thus I was keeping up with Tommy Parker. Tommy Parker was a fan of ice-hockey at the time, even when the only games being played were in Australia.

Arthurson said "I read the other day that a latest form of psychiatric treatment makes provision for alleviating repression not by the remembering of the original scene in the mind but by re-enacting it positively this time in the present. Before I admit my particular neurosis I want to make sure there are these arrangements at Oxford."

Tommy Parker said "Overtime for mums." He often made his jokes in the form of newspaper headlines.

Most of our jokes are elliptical things, playing leap-frog with our minds, leaving out connecting sentences. Some of us make a joke of being up to date and some of being out of date; but we all have to make these jokes, because then we can move away from a subject quickly like birds from a carcase, being guilty about being so cut off. We have our work which is serious and our social life which is not: and our outside life is different. I have no friends in college. No real friends. There is something inimical to them.

About our work, it is something that seems to me at a certain stage to take over and live a life of its own. At the beginning it is a matter of your managing it with difficulty; then it is just there, you don't have to worry much any more. But by now it has become something that you need; your personality. You are in a group, with dependence upon the system. You stop asking what relevance all this has to anything else. Except in these jokes, of course; or in the middle of the night. Or when something comes in from outside to destroy it.

I think Oxford is conducive to all this; a very old place there for the young—old men, buildings, ways, for something which has nothing to do with them, and which they can only deal with by defeating. What else can the old do to the young? Sometimes at Oxford you come across a scene of extraordinary beauty—deer in front of an eighteenth century facade, trees growing out of the water of the river—and you stop to watch; and all around you there is the roar of traffic, dim at first, then growing; the blossom and the grass and the traffic pressed tight around Oxford in a circle of smoking vehicles like an army. I do not know what one makes of all this—we understand now only workings and not meanings. The traffic is undermining the structure of the buildings and the buildings crumble. Against this background we—the teachers—talk, move with our profiles and our long gowns flowing. We are looking at something else, in the distance. We are not seen much as persons any more; rather as guardians, priests in a jungle. We begin to look like this; knowledgeable and deathly. What we guard is true. But no one asks us what it is. The clearing in the jungle.

6.

Anna sat with her notebook on her knees and her knees close together. I walked between the bookcase, the window. I said "But this is a criticism of the whole method. A purely rational system is either faulty or sterile. It can go back to a position of certainty about existence, but from this point it has to introduce empiricism in order to describe what exists. About the self, for instance, it can say that something exists because there is something that thinks it exists, but it can't say if this something has either substance or identity or continuity without appealing to experience."

Anna said "Then what's the point?"

I said "It has clarified this point about the scope and function."

Anna did that disbelieving look going sideways around the room.

I said "But then, in fact, you find much the same sort of thing. If you look into your experience you find a succession of impressions of, for instance, thinking, desiring, hoping, fearing; but you don't have a continued impression of a self that thinks or desires or hopes or fears. So the description of the self as an enduring entity is again impossible."

Anna said "Then what is?"

I said "A possible way to talk about the self?"

Anna said "Yes."

I said "You can analyse the way in which we actually do talk. But this of course is not an answer to the original question."

A big girl in a long green dress. Her hair done up. Looking Dutch, with pink cheeks and round cheekbones.

Anna said "But surely people have been trying to find an answer. I mean writers and artists and so on."

I said "Of course anyone can give his own answer. But you can't give an answer that will be generally acceptable."

Anna said "Even a great writer?"

I said "It's true that art is the medium to offer answers, but these will of course be outside the scope of reason, which is all that can actually prove anything."

Anna stared at her notebook. I had not really noticed her before. I wanted to engrave her. Memory.

I said "Do you see the point?"

Anna said "Not really."

I said "If you're not the sort of person who wants to do this, don't."

Anna said "I do."

I sat down. Put my feet on a stool. Confident.

Anna said "But it only seems to analyse and separate, it doesn't build."

I said "You clear the ground."

She said "What I mean is—" Stopped.

I said "What you mean is, what relation have the things we're talking about to what actually we do, the way we behave."

She said "Yes."

Hostile look. Big blowsy face like a barmaid.

I said "You can say this of anyone."

She said "But people don't talk about it any more."

I said "I do."

She said "Do you?"

Philosophers are on the defensive. My smile like an Indian.

She said "I suppose it's inevitable that everything seems so empty and unconstructive."

I said "This is a certain kind of truth. Do you want to impose on it?"

She said "No."

I said "Once it was all dreams, any old nonsense. We were obsessed by this. Now we know. And it's a good thing we do, because now it would be too dangerous. It's reason, at least, that keeps the world going."

She said "It may not keep going."

I said "Oh that!" I jerked my head.

She said "What?"

I said "Well yes, but at least now we've got choice. Before it was just accident."

She said "It can still be accident."

I said "Your generation is obsessed by this. You think the world's going to blow up. That life has been unfair to you. I don't feel this. I feel responsibility is better."

She said nothing.

I said "The world is tough. No one up till now has thought it wasn't."

She said "All this is very different from my essay."

I said "We're not all distant academics."

She put a rubber band round her notebook.

I said "For next week write me something in your

sort of language. On what you think is the problem."

She said "The problem of personal identity?"

I said "If you like."

She said "You'll think it terrible."

I said "That doesn't matter."

After she had gone I tried to remember what I had felt about her. I could visualise her fairly well. Her green skirt and notebook. I wondered if I had flirted with her. Philosophers are not so clever when on the attack. Motives are different from actions. There is the putting forward of an idea, an event. Being unfair. Leaving the person to do what they like with it.

7.

I remember one Sunday about this time (what is a story? a sequence? meaning?) when I went with my wife Rosalind and the children to the Wiltshire downs, driving on a windy spring day to a country of flint and fir plantations, a white land with rain running off it, hard country with cold air. It was the time of some international crisis—Cuba, I suppose, or it must have been before—and there was the feeling glimpsed over the shoulder of death, of those bright men with their machines already buried. We climbed up a long slope with me carrying Clarissa on my back and Alexander picking up white stones to keep them; and I thought of that fire, that blast to nothingness, the world disappearing like a conjuror. I loved my family; there was something marvellous in it; this thing created, held, the four of us—Clarissa with her gold hair and bright black eyes, Alexander with his dream of forgotten continents, my wife Rosalind whom I adored. It was only sometimes I knew this—love, that other part of me, that I was pierced with an arrow to. Her grave eyes and long gold neck; Rosalind. We turned to the view at the top of the hill and there was the world below, valley and village. Compact in its nest, womb. Hardly born yet.

I said—"I've been talking to my pupils, some of them, what they feel. There is a sort of agony in it. They just see any violence, death, being wrong. They don't think any more of rights, or duties, or motives."

Rosalind said "Who have you been talking to?"

I said "I wonder if we ought to do something. I'm almost forty now. People become characters at forty. They stop. They don't feel anything".

Rosalind was unhappy. She did not like me talking like this. The hill was cold. Huge black clouds rushed on the surface.

I cried "Don't turn away!"

She said "What do you mean we ought to do?"

I said "These people know something. They're spontaneous. They have no defences."

Rosalind with her pale tired face. Her coat blown over her womb, her baby.

I knelt down and picked up a chalk stone. I threw it.

I said "I know you've got the baby, darling."

She said "Isn't it all right?"

I said (as I so often said) "We know about this. People do feel dried up, unemotional. I don't know if it's age, or the bomb, or what. I don't want any of the ordinary things.

33

I don't want to drink, be ambitious, to have affairs. I've got this problem. It doesn't matter much."

She said "You've got the children."

I said "I said I've got the children!"

Being pregnant, she was often on the edge of tears. Hanging over a precipice.

I picked up Clarissa and whirled her round, waltzing.

I said to Alexander "Race you to the fir trees and back!"

We set off at a run, across the hard earth, Alexander in front, elbows out, Clarissa on my back with her head pressed tight against my shoulder.

Alexander shouted "I won!"

I said to Rosalind "Don't be sad, my love, you know what I care about, you, you and the children, just a little about my work, nothing else. But we've got to talk. Nothing stays still. There's an emptiness perhaps in a lot of people, now, perhaps me, in quite a new way. It's nothing to do with love, or the children; but a sort of gap between us and the world, you know, all that mystical rubbish—" I knelt and patted my hand on the earth—"You know how I hate it!" I screwed my face up. "But it's true!" I found myself still kneeling.

Rosalind said "I feel too close. Sometimes everything seems rushing outwards, as if one more thing would break it."

I thought—I had wanted to talk about Anna. Say—This is the conversation I had with a pupil the other day.

Rosalind said "I had a dream the other night. I was being trampled by a crowd of people panicking."

I stood and put my arm around her. Those forbidden things—love, tenderness.

I said "I was just talking."

Rosalind put her cheek on my shoulder. We folded our wings inwards. Clarissa, whom I was still carrying, put her head against ours. We were three circles touching. Then Alexander, from where he clung to Rosalind's skirt, had to be lifted, heaved, on to this tripod of emotions—into our arms, our joint arms, so that we would be together in the air like acrobats, a moment a festoon. This thing that made life worth living—feet, legs, thighs, earth, sex. I thought —We will make love tonight. Then I remembered the child, tender as pain. Rosalind hard with tree and muscle. This pyramid of living things: straining upwards. Holding it in our hands. Trembling.

III

8.

WE sometimes go to parties in Oxford which are dreadful things in the Woodstock Road with a room cleared of carpets and bottles of wine in a Victorian bow window.

I enter. Nod against the noise like royalty being explained machinery.

William was there: a war-hero, both legs shattered, plastic surgery around his soul.

Tommy Parker was there: in all-black strip, laced boots, about to run on blowing a whistle.

A marvellous blonde girl with her back to me: long hair, from the waist down, no stockings.

I do not like parties. I say this while I am going, after I have left, while I am there. Undergraduates and the party-going dons and the art crowd. A woman in a Shakespearian helmet. Noise and rubble. I am always moving across the room to talk to someone else. I never do. Or on the defensive, looking animals in the eye. They do not jump.

I was yelling at the woman in the helmet. About opium. She had spectacles fluted like an early railway engine.

My wife Rosalind, pale, with long gold earrings, was

talking to William. She was saying "Go and see Danilo Dolci."

William tapped his cigarette. A one-legged man in an alley.

I thought—I am too old for this. I am going bald. My teeth hurt. I wear glasses.

There was a commotion by the door as a group of people came in. Someone shouted "My brother!" It was Charlie.

Charlie is not my brother; but he is sometimes taken to be because we look alike, being tall and thin and intellectual. Charlie pushed into the room carrying an umbrella. He looked like a corpse. He said "I just happened to be passing." He put a hand on Rosalind's shoulder. He began laughing. When we are with Charlie we always begin laughing. He is our joker. Our familiar.

He said "Are you coming to the antipodes?"

I said "Yes."

Charlie peered round. He was unshaven. His face was white and tired. He crossed the room to the marvellous looking girl with long hair who had her back to us. He put his hand on her shoulder. The girl turned. It was Anna.

I thought—But I didn't recognise Anna!

Charlie said "Are you coming to the antipodes?"

Anna's skirt was short, like something you skated in. A bit of fur. The ice wet.

Charlie shouted "No, I didn't think you were someone else!"

Something old in memory, a golden age with satyrs and nymphs and fauns.

Charlie came back across the room and started saying "There was this advertisement in the *Times* for a party to go to—"

37

Charlie stammers. He ceases in mid-sentence and stands with his mouth open and his eyes closed like a child being given medicine.

"To the antipodes" I said.

"No no no!" Charlie yelled.

He shut his eyes again.

He was carrying his umbrella and a box of matches. Rosalind took the box of matches out of his hand, lit a cigarette, and put the box of matches back in his hand.

Charlie said in a deep fluent voice "Hullo my dear, that's a nice new dress you're wearing, did you make it?"

"Did you make your umbrella?" Rosalind said.

Charlie doubled up and began walking round the room with his head close to the floor. He passed close to Anna, who was watching him.

A magic circle on the grass. Charlie. A ring of fire.

Charlie came back to us. He said "Look!" He lifted his umbrella, and it opened slowly of its own accord.

"Japanese!" Charlie shouted.

Rosalind put her hand round the umbrella and tried to close it. She said "It's dangerous!"

William had split some of his drink. He was screwing it on the boards with his foot.

Charlie began again. "There was this advertisement in *The Times* for some people to go and dig a deep shelter in the the—" He was leaning with one hand on Rosalind's shoulder and the other on the umbrella. After a time he went on "I went to see him and—"

The woman in the spectacles said "You two boys going to the antipodes?"

Charlie opened his eyes and stared at her.

No one else was thinking this funny. I don't know why we thought it funny. Charlie's hair was standing on end. Rosalind and I were rolling about.

"He had a pick—" Charlie said.

"A what?" Rosalind said.

"A pick," Charlie shouted.

The group of undergraduates with Anna had come over. They stood around not looking.

Charlie had taken out a packet of cigarettes. I knew what he was going to do. He pulled off the silver paper, gave the piece of cardboard a jerk, and all the cigarettes flew out on to the floor.

Charlie squatted and began picking up the cigarettes. They were all around Anna's feet. He said "I beg your pardon."

Anna squatted and began helping him.

Anna looked different with her hair down. Swedish. Thin. Dreaming into the sun.

Charlie said "What did you say your name was?"

He put his ear close to her mouth. Screwed his face up, showing a black tooth with silver round it.

Charlie shouted "Eh?"

To balance himself he put his wrist on Anna's knee.

"Never been there!" Charlie shouted.

He was pushing the cigarettes and silver paper back into the packet. They went in crooked and bits of tobacco were squashed out at the other end.

Charlie said "Has anyone got a cigarette?"

I was introducing Anna to Rosalind. That odd moment when they touch.

Charlie began talking fluently to Rosalind. He said "Can

I possibly come and stay with you tonight? I was really going somewhere quite different." He had his back to Anna.

"Have you brought your own food?" Rosalind said.

Charlie said to one of the undergraduates "Once when I came to stay with them I happened to have a packet of—"

The undergraduate was frowning.

I thought—Are we really so awful? People hate us.

I said "Do stay."

Charlie said "—cucumber sandwiches."

William was trying to talk to Anna: Anna looking down, her face crooked as William's sometimes was. Charlie and I were collapsing. There was this thing objectionable about happiness: it was so vulgar. I felt I was young again. A boy camping out, in the morning.

Later that night when Rosalind had gone to bed Charlie arrived and came through the hall and dining room that was like a passage and found me in the sitting room with the yellow carpet and black curtains. He was groaning and scratching his head. He said—"I've been drunk for three days. Why do we do it"?

When he is drunk or talking to you on your own he does not stammer. He sometimes seems to be talking to himself; making up a story.

He said "I went up to London, I'd been working in the country a long time, wanted to have a binge, you know, all that stuff. Domesticity and work. If you don't do it what else do you do, you know, how to keep lively."

Charlie acts what he is saying with pauses, gestures. The way he can manage it.

"So I went up to London to this club, a drinking club,

you know, and sat, just sat there, like millions do it. And there was this girl, a big dark girl, on a bench, reading Balzac. I asked her why she was reading Balzac. Of all things. I said she must be insane. You know I love Balzac. After that we got on very well. A girl who liked modern art and all that stuff. I said it was too photographic. Would you believe it. God!" Charlie strode around as if in pain.

I said "Where is this club?"

Charlie said "I'll tell you."

He went on "So there we were, everything laid on, drinks, dinner, out in the street. Then—Why don't you come home and have some coffee? I mean she said that, I didn't. And up to a house in Hampstead, brown wallpaper, land-lady, Indians, the lot. She began telling me the story of her life. She'd been married to an Italian who'd thrown her through a plate glass window. She'd been to school at Cheltenham. Her father was a major. She was living with a pimp in Hampstead."

I thought—I'm too tired. I've been working.

I said "And then what?"

"She said, Would you like to stay? I said I wouldn't mind. She said, You go on upstairs. I went upstairs. There were two children. In a cot. With teddy bears."

I thought—This is terrible. Why is he telling me all this?

I said "What happened?"

Charlie said "Nothing. Morals aren't an exhortation, they're a fact."

I laughed. I thought—This is a good story after all.

Charlie said "She said she didn't want love, only sex. I said I did too. She said But do you love your wife? I said

Of course I love my wife. She said Then why are you here?
I said Of course I'm here."

I said "And nothing happened?"

Charlie said "No."

I said "You're stuck with it."

9.

Charlie is my greatest friend. He is a writer. He lives in Wiltshire, with a wife and three children.

Charlie is working class. At least he says he is. He says he has a grandfather who was on the railway and an uncle who is doorman at the Ritz. We were once driving past the Ritz and Charlie leaned out of the window and called "Uncle!" but he hit his head on a lamp post and was knocked unconscious.

I do not know how to write about Charlie. We describe best people who mean nothing to us—as a thing, an object. People we love we can't bring alive. Novels are usually about people we don't like, because we can portray them so clearly and deathly.

Charlie's father had been some sort of clerk in the civil service. Charlie had got scholarships to schools but when he was sixteen had run away and played the saxophone in a dance band. His mother and father had worked their fingers to the bone. His mother and father were quite well off in Worthing. The thing about the dance band must have been true, because there is a photograph of him at this time sitting in the back row of something called The White Peppers, looking like Harold Lloyd.

When I first met Charlie he was still something like this, his hair falling down each side of his face and an expression as if someone were coming up behind him. He had a blurred accent. It is difficult now to remember this. We had both come to Oxford on scholarships, Charlie having worked for his on his mornings off from The White Peppers. This was during the early part of the war, our call-up deferred.

After the war we took up at Oxford again but both so much older. Charlie was now wearing smart clothes suddenly with thin trousers and a bowler hat. No one else was doing this. Before the war he had worn pink shirts and bow ties, which everyone else was now doing. He had lost his accent.

Charlie was living with a much older woman in London who came down to see him at weekends dressed in a fur coat and very high heeled shoes. I remember her coming past the porter's lodge and struggling across the lawn like someone in a blizzard. Charlie would begin swearing and groaning. Her footsteps would come up interminable wooden stairs, and Charlie would climb out of the window.

I remember this time of my life very well. But we change too much; it's not ourselves that we remember. Charlie and I had one of those undergraduate friendships that are like love; very selfish. We were both supposed to be in love at some time with the wife of a psychologist who kept a salon in Walton Street. We were in love with ourselves. We each had an affair with her. Then years later I met her and she was mad, with hair like Alice-in-Wonderland.

Charlie was modelling himself on Julien Sorel: I (or Charlie) on someone in Dostoievsky.

Looking back on it it is easy to impose a pattern on all this; Charlie breaking away from his past into first the cautious boy with the blurred accent watching, learning things; then the person who had learned the value of being odd, a personality. Charlie says his stammer has something to do with this; you have to rely on something other than speech, some understanding. But we all try to do this. I think it is people who are very selfish at this age who have a sort of magic.

Charlie missed his first-class degree. The older woman he lived with began committing suicide.

Charlie had begun writing at Oxford. He grew into one of those lost generations of writers like the lost politicians from the first world war—mostly dead, or if they were not a feeling that they should be. He wrote a play called *Palm Tuesday* which was the sort of thing fashionable during those years after the war—in verse with a bit of music and rather religious and no politics. I remember the prompter coming on to the stage and waving his script about. It was not a very good play, and is difficult to read now, but it got Charlie a certain fame. He was the only playwright of the time to achieve some gossip: the others were respectable. Charlie stayed quite famous till about 1955, when the thing changed and playwrights became hardworking people caring about class and money. Charlie by this time had married the daughter of a millionaire.

Laura was a pupil at the Royal School of Music. She wore brightly coloured shirts, black trousers, and spectacles with up-slanting rims. She played the piano with her head curiously close to the music.

It has only just struck me how like Anna Laura was. Big,

with those sort of clothes. Rather immobile, as short-sighted people are. One falls in love with either a type, or its opposite.

Laura was heiress to a shipping fortune. Her father had objected to Charlie and had locked Laura up in Northumberland so they were married in a Chelsea registry office. (I find myself writing, speaking like Charlie: we copy one another.) By this time Charlie had given up his bowler hat and had a horsey appearance, wearing tweed jackets and what were called cavalry twill trousers. He was soon on the best of terms with the millionaire, shooting and fishing in Scotland.

All this seems rather out of date now. Charlie wrote two novels that did not sell very well: then a volume of essays and a travel book about Spain. Then he became a reviewer for *The Observer*. People said how sad it was, that he had become a reviewer for *The Observer*.

I did not see much of Charlie then. I was unmarried; and there is that thing about men's friendship being difficult after one has married. We had been very close; there was also the shame as well as the nostalgia. Men's friendships are like war, glorious and infantile.

When I married myself the whole thing changed back again (or just we grew older; I was a junior fellow of St. Mark's now, teaching these people that Charlie and I had been a few years ago; but with their seriousness now, their smiles instead of giggles) and I thought of seeing Charlie again as I so often talked about him; and my wife Rosalind wanted to meet such a reviewer on *The Observer*. So we all did meet. Charlie now went to a very expensive tailor and seemed to be carrying a gun in a shoulder-holster. Laura was in a black woollen dress very fashionable. I remember Rosalind being pregnant.

I wish I could say what I mean about all this. There are two things, first, that people are not characters but things moving occasionally in jumps and mostly in indiscernible slowness: and secondly, the opposite, that we had each of us in a way got what we wanted; so that we were at rest now though unwillingly, a sort of violent rest like a ping-pong ball. Charlie had his rich wife and his position as Sunday journalist (perhaps he still wanted to be a great writer; perhaps he was): I had (for all I know I am talking of myself) much the same. We were young middle-aged intellectuals, young rather marvellous wives. We all became great friends again. In some ancient ring-a-roses.

I might always be writing of myself. Charlie might be writing this story. My father was a schoolmaster; my step-mother someone with tea and biscuits. I sometimes wanted to murder them. Of course, in the unconscious.

Rosalind was a tall girl seen through statues.

10.

William appeared half round the door of my room and hung there, charmingly, on a hook. He said—"Working?"

I said "Come in, come in."

This must have been about a third of the way through term. Hot. Everything arms and legs, open windows, traffic. William wore a white shirt to the waist. He said— "This Anna von Graz."

I said "Oh dear oh dear".

I thought—I'm becoming a joke.

He said "I asked her for a weekend home. She won't come."

I said "Good girl." I cleared my throat to make it less ridiculous.

"It must be some custom where she comes from."

"If you think that—" A favourite expression.

"I wondered if you could ask us both to Palling. Is this sherry?"

An English summer evening. Bats, balls, and men in dark panelling. Had been like this for centuries.

"What's wrong with that sherry?"

"I thought dons were supposed to be connoisseurs of wines."

I sipped, I clicked with my tongue, looked at the ceiling. Charlie had a routine in which he swallowed, held the glass up, put his finger in it, screamed, and wrapped a handkerchief round his finger.

I said "You want me—"

"Ask us both to Palling."

"For the weekend?"

"Oh, just the day. What can I bribe you with?"

That Spanish man in the sherry advertisement. Narrow eyes. Frilled shirt. A woman.

I said "Why'd she come to Palling and not to you?"

"Oh she's such a great opinion of you!"

I said "Oh ho!"

"She asked about you. Where you lived, what your wife was like."

William was from a military family. A fourth generation

aristocrat. Living vicariously. Having learned it at Eton and Oxford.

I said "All right I'll ask her."

"You'll quite like her."

"Of course I'll like her!"

"Thank you so much. When?"

I had not thought much about Anna. Girls are girls, in the streets, in the shops, in cafés. You watch them, wonder. Occasionally they come up the wooden stairs to your room and are nervous, and young, their legs close together. They read their essays in soft jerking voices. You day-dream. Nothing peculiar.

I said "I'll fix it."

William said "Shall I give you the address of my wine merchant?"

He was pretending to mean it. Pretending to pretend to mean it. I thought—Charlie and I would have once learned from William. By mirrors.

II.

Anna sat with her knees at an angle and her legs close together. I said—"Read that sentence again."

Anna read—"An act of freedom breaking away from the limits of acceptance develops into commitment as well as rebellion, and it is this with which a person can identify himself. The statement 'I will' is at once a realisation that something exists within and yet there is something opposing it without."

I banged my pipe against a bowl, see-sawed, stretched my eyes, said "Oh well oh well oh well, what is that, Sartre, Camus, I suppose."

She was wearing a green dress, hair done up, blousy again.

She said "I do—" Then looked embarrassed.

I said "The trouble is this is like poetry, private language, you can't analyse it. In what sense do you use the word freedom or rebellion or anything. The meaning is only in a state of mind, in which words are not doing much anyway."

Anna said "There's something in poetry."

I said "Now less than ever. Your generation should see this, who are so practical and unmythical."

Anna said "Are we?"

I said "Let's go back. If I ask what are the ways you use the word 'I' or 'myself' you use other words about which I can ask the same questions. You don't look for words about which I might not have to ask these questions. But this is the point of philosophy."

Anna seemed about to tumble out of her clothes, her stockings. Wisps of hair.

I said "Never mind. I told you to write that sort of essay."

She closed her notebook. Started putting a rubber band around it.

I said "For this week—" I squatted in front of my books. Millions of books. Words. Squeezed with exhausting effort.

She said "Why do you always say my generation?"

I said "Don't you think so?"

She said "No."

I said "I should have thought you all had this distrust of

ideals and emotions, you're only interested in techniques."

She said "We're not."

I said "My generation was involved in ideals because of the war and the thirties, though in philosophy of course we were obsessed with techniques." I felt nervous. "Perhaps that's why in philosophy your generation likes so much hot air."

Anna said "You make out we're so different."

I try to remember how she said this. The actor's back to the camera. The shot held. I misunderstood it.

I said "Of course we're all like this. Having driven out the one devil we've got seven more." I tried to analyse why I was nervous.

The actor holding the whole stage. The nerves outside him.

I said "Would you like to come to my house on Sunday?"

I had gone and knelt by the bookcase, had had my back to her, had talked, in order to say this.

"That would be lovely," Anna said.

"You could meet my wife."

"Yes."

I looked at my books. I sometimes hated books. I thought of non-books, thrillers. I wanted to be ill enough to read them.

I said "We live just outside."

She said "I know."

I thought—William must have told her.

I said "Do you want any books?"

She squatted down beside me. In front of a fire with our hands out.

I saw the book of essays by Charlie called *The Wrong*

Rebellion. I took it out and began thumbing through the pages. I said "Now here you are! This is your thing!"

Anna held the book. She had long beautiful fingers.

I said "Charlie's a romantic!" I put a hand to the floor to stop myself overbalancing.

I said "You met him the other day at the party."

She turned to the title page. I looked over her shoulder. Opposite Charlie's name and that of the publisher there was the rather affected quotation that Charlie had put there from Nietzsche: *If you want to prepossess someone in your favour then you must be embarrassed in front of him.*

12.

In a punt beneath overhanging branches in some caricature of an Oxford summer with blazers and hats, tinfoil and water, butterflies and lances; William and Anna in a white dress and parasol, he with his sleeves rolled up. I had been walking along the towpath by the meadow where they had once planned to build a tunnel (the green fields and cows and willows not only surrounded by traffic but undermined; one ventilator in the middle like a volcano or entrance to hell) and had come across them thus, William and Anna, in a punt. I leaned down to talk; the shape of willow (I don't know about trees) like water falling, fern and rock, leg from the hip and bark and silver. The heat was a sound, a dropping of chestnuts. In front of me there was a white parasol and brown boat and blue velvet cushions. William said "Come and join us!" Anna had brown legs with curiously dented hollows. I was wearing black walking shoes. Around me were those pinpoints of light in pure colour; waterweeds and mountain, sky and shadow, mauve and viridian. Anna was wearing a white dress like a mosquito net. We get these impressions less and less—summer teeming with leaves, heat, wasps, jungle; a sort of ache in the soul, an ecstasy. I said "You've got room?" Anna was golden, a girl in the wind. I stepped in and the boat rocked. William pushed off. He was crouched at the knees, a man at a tournament. I was down on the blue velvet with that touch, smell, of childhood. Varnished wood and dust, stickiness. Men with moustaches. White net and parasols. I knelt by Anna.

I wish I had been able to understand all this; myself ungainly, on hands and knees, by Anna's legs. In the position of some old prisoner, Jew (difficult to say this); something archetypal in wrong clothes, boots, a mop and pail, a number. Looking up with that look we've grown accustomed to but even now do not quite believe; of terrible numbness and passivity. What was evil then? And outside me that seethingness of summer; the bright wood, blue velvet, water and trees (I say this again); the golden age, absolute, with couples and shining faces. Anna's dress was in minutely woven holes infinitely complex. My elbows and knees were on the hard wood; between them, in the sun, something like a stem, green. I had forgotten this. As William pushed the boat shot forwards. A movement solid, rocking, like a wooden horse. I myself shook, as if having a small fit.

We forget the way in which this particular, love, goes out at moments to mingle with that other universal, world; the faces keening, streaming seesaw in the wind. Myself shaking in front of a sort of earth mother, Anna, white dress, carved gold legs, green stem, Procris and Venus. That grave black dog. Anna a Renoir, a Scurat by the river, William in mediaeval Florence. Raising my tired eyes—for ten thousand years spitting, bearded—at that patch, through leaves. On my elbow and hip. Reclining.

William, pushing on his punt-pole, went gliding up the Cherwell, Isis, Thames, the Grand Canal at Venice. Beneath low branches the boat was a bird. By my side, half way down her thigh, Anna. My head on the level of her arms. I faced her way, so that we both looked at William. He was moving up and down with his pole. Anna's lower half was directly in front of me, her legs crossed, myself body, hip, thighs, torso. There was a vapour on her hair, on muscle. Alchemists saw life in globes, crystals. I did not want to lose all this. I took deep breaths. The seeds of the trees came down like parachutes. There was invasion. The child turned to its mother's lap. The boat shot over the water. We seemed to be coming towards some island; mysterious.

13.

It was about this time I started becoming extraordinarily greedy. I remembered a joke—The only pleasure you can get three times a day till you're eighty. An old man with tiny eyes glinting.

When I woke in the morning there was something that I looked forward to, and it was breakfast.

Driving into Oxford along the dual carriage way with

trees uprooted, I wondered if there was anything permanent in our lives. That we could do about it.

Moving past the walls of college in the morning light my legs thin, my gown, my shadow flowing, I sometimes wanted to become like this entirely, an eccentric with rumpled clothes and skin with stuffing. To say—I give up, get it over with.

Moving through the arches of a club into the masculine world, exclusive, personalities like shaving sticks. Guarding against the terrible rush outside of grass, leaves, beetles, women.

I have an office downstairs where I do college business. I look at letters about admissions to the college from schools, public schools, schoolmasters, parents. I dictate to a secretary. I say—In reply to your letter of the—. To offer you a place in the—. What have I said? We keep the air, the summer out. There is the roar of the blossom falling and the lilac. I become the prisoner again. I say—I can offer you—. Sincerely.

The old have their revenge upon the young. Lock them up in beautiful walls and crumbling buildings.

Once Rosalind and I had been young. We had lived in one room and had had no possessions.

I go up a narrow white staircase to a sort of tower. I feel accustomed in my room. There are oak pillars, fire, chair, bookcase. What I am making myself into. My surroundings. Millstones and necklaces.

For elevenses the dons meet in a room like an Aberystwyth boarding house. We shoot into it like balls on a pin table. We bounce to different corners, centrifugally. We put our papers up. Everyone has a paper. We wrap our minds in it like old fish.

The Provost of St. Mark's is an ex-diplomat who had been ambassador in, say, Rome, and who was elected as a compromise between two candidates more suitable. A tall bald man with hooded eyes who listens to you in a sort of trance and then comes to with a jerk and a comment of no relevance. He stands in front of the empty fireplace with his fingers on his hips pointing downwards. In front of him are a dozen huge men like schoolboys.

He said "Stephen! Recovered? From your rite of spring?"

I took ten seconds to get this. The day before, with Anna and William, I had fallen into the river.

I laughed.

I sometimes thought of murdering the Provost. Why dons write detective stories.

Tommy Parker said "Von Graz is quite a dish."

I could get my own back on Tommy Parker. His name would come up for some administrative post, and I would vote against him.

Arthurson said "What was the temperature?"

The Provost said "Do you know the story of Provost Jones and the punt pole?"

We rustled our papers. Leaves in a dead autumn.

The Provost said "Oh surely—"

Provost Jones was a mythical figure who had been head of college two or three incarnations ago. He had been a character, an old man like a monkey, whom everyone loved and mocked.

"Provost Jones was out punting one day with his good lady . . ."

I had been in the boat with William and Anna when we

had come to the island. I had tried to climb out on to a tree. The tree was difficult because the trunk was so broad. I could hardly get my arms around it. I had been holding on to it like a bear. I had fallen in. I had had to walk back along the High Street.

". . . and left him behind, as was inevitable, on the punt-pole . . ."

The trouble with murder was not clues, but conscience. The Provost was a smooth phallic man who if you topped him would grow again like a space-carrot. Once when I was young I had had an affair with his daughter. She had been a dark girl called Francesca, who had rushed about with her eyes half closed as if in a sort of panic. She had told me that once, when she was fifteen, her father had made a pass at her in the bath. He had been sitting on the lavatory.

". . . and Provost Jones said 'A direct refutation of Darwin'."

I said to Tommy Parker "What was that?"

Tommy Parker said "Direct refutation of Darwin."

A tall, vegetable figure. Diplomat. The dark girl in despair, running, running. Or had she imagined it?

I could not see the point of the Provost's story. Provost Jones had been left on the punt pole. Darwin.

That morning we went to yet another room, a dining room, to have a committee. We had then committees once a fortnight during term, to discuss college business. Moving in single file down stone corridors, I thought—I will go to some primitive country and work there with my hands. A white house with fruit trees. We were all on the edge of some universal catastrophe. Devils coming down with their horns. The committee would be endless.

My daughter, Clarissa.

Leather chairs scratched round the edges with iron files. I thought—I am becoming ill.

The Provost knocked on the table. We were about to enjoy this. At the time of the revolution we ticked off names to be guillotined. This was our routine. Money and power.

I thought—A lot of dons get ill around forty. Their great minds tick over like Big Ben. Then the whole works suddenly flips over, an arm gone berserk, the weights in free fall to the basement. Holding a toe. Screaming.

The Provost was making a speech.

I thought—I will remember this room. When I am one of the inmates. Dead. Or buried. The Provost, Tommy Parker, Arthurson and myself. We will not be dug up for two thousand years.

IV

14.

THE side of my house that faces towards the village is bordered by a stone wall within which is a garden of rose-beds and a lawn. I had planted roses with their lovely names—Madame Laparrière, Marcelle Gret, Mary Wheatcroft—digging, spreading the roots out, treading the earth. In the winter there had been cold and the grit of bone: I had been a soldier in my loose overcoat and the barbed wire. I had worked in no-man's land till the lights came on; asked what am I doing, why I am doing it. Going into the house to wife, children, fire, boots, hearthrug.

Then in the spring there had been the first purple shoots from the sticks so slight a razor might cut them. I moved over the earth with a hoe like Adam in tears. Doing some penance for what he did not know, had never asked for.

In the summer the leaves and buds came and the weeds that I destroyed, a scavenger on hands and knees pulling at soft stalks and bodies. Throwing them into some communal grave, a charnel house.

At this side of my house beyond the grey stone wall is a footpath which is the quickest way to the village. When I am gardening I do not want to be seen. I get into the shadow of the wall, pale rough stones laid flat with earth, and watch the bees with antennae like pianos. Footsteps from the other side come up from the village.

Bees look for honey from wisps of moss. Touch of aubretia.

Footsteps stop. Someone sneezes just above me.

I do not enter much into village life. The village is a group of cottages round the pub and church in the hollow. Sometimes the vicar comes up the path to have a talk with me, his head and shoulders moving above the wall like a target on a funfair shooting range.

A sneeze again. A laugh. I am crouching on my knees in the shadow.

"Hullo, Stephen, Stephen, what are you doing?" Very quietly.

"Hullo Vicar!"

"Getting out more now in the summer?"

Caught in the light of a flare. No fly buttons.

"I wonder, Stephen, if you could do something . . ."

No.

"Of course!"

"Read the lessons in church on Sunday."

The vicar has a huge dead face gone absolutely white, rather beautiful. Somewhere soft blue eyes with pain spilled over them.

"I'm sorry, I think we've got people coming."

"I wish you would, it'd be a great favour."

His church is grey stone with a squat tower. The people who go are from the few big houses round about. The village stays away and makes up stories about him.

"I'll see."

"I'd be so grateful!"

Supposed to have seduced someone in the Sunday school. Accused of inhuman treatment of cats.

"Our people may not be coming until lunch."

"I'll ring you. Have you got a Bible?"

"I think so."

"Jolly good!"

What had gone wrong? A good man.

"Well!" he jumped.

The awful cold church in the dark.

He said "I suppose I couldn't persuade you, Stephen, to come on the council?"

I said "I don't really believe."

He said "I sometimes wonder if that matters."

"So do I." I laughed.

The good brown earth in my hands. Once this would have been a thing of tension; bells and music. Now we act it all so slowly. The camera stays for minutes on a close-up. Speaks for itself. Silence. Time running out.

I think I am only writing this because of that permanent point in time where Anna lies with her hair out, one arm raised, on the four-poster in our spare room. Her skirt like a bell and her legs parallel. Myself like mad Fuseli, dark face and rolling eyes somewhere above her.

I am looking back on all this not to explain it, nor describe it, but to say what it means. Incomprehensible. But what else? Choices.

Anna with her white dresses and green jerseys and tartan skirts. She was never beautiful. We were fascinated because of that nothingness about her, so that we could put anything we liked on to her. William had said—What do you make of her? Charlie said—What was she like? We questioned each other—out of interest. There was something we each wanted. Moments took on a particular meaning.

Myself like Othello, standing above Desdemona.

At what point did the course of events go wrong? In my room in front of the bookcase, in the punt, in the hot grass with the reek of pollen. In the corridors of William's house.

An accident is different from reality.

Rosalind foreshadowed it. Pregnant women and lunatics and gypsies.

Anna lying in the bed after William's death. My wife Rosalind lying there in summer. But she had to fight in a limited area of her own. Not prevent it.

"Darling—"

"Yes?"

"What are you doing?"

"Trying to rest. You can hear everything in the front of the house."

On the four-poster. The curtains drawn. A blanket.

"Beloved—"

"Yes?"

"I've asked some people over on Sunday."

No answer. I stood at the foot of the bed.

"Darling—"

"Yes?"

"Are you all right?"

She stirred. The edge of a blanket over her mouth. Going puffy round the eyes and temples.

"I'm all right. Who are they?"

"Well William, who you know."

"Yes."

"And this Anna von Graz."

Silence again. I leaned and pulled the blanket down from her mouth. Her face from a distant country.

I said "Only for lunch, we can go out if you like, or I'll help with the cooking."

She said "It's not the cooking."

I said "What is it then?"

One of the children began to cry in the garden. She lifted her head. To the smell of water.

I said "Don't pay attention!"

She said "I feel so awful."

I thought—One day I may leave her. Perhaps she will die.

I said "I'll put them off." Beneath the canopy of the four-poster.

She said "No don't put them off."

"I don't like you in this room. It's not like you."

"You will look after me?"

"Of course I'll look after you."

"I sometimes feel you may—" She was crying.

"What?"

What was in our minds? What put things in our minds; dreams; experience.

"You may just go off—"

"And leave you?" I laughed.

"Yes."

I put my hand against hers. Stroked it. I said "You know what this is, just the baby."

She said "But you won't will you?"

I said "Of course I won't!"

She put an arm up and held me. How odd my voice had been.

She said "Good."

The children were in the garden. The curtains were drawn in the afternoon. I was impatient.

15.

On the very few occasions we go to church we move around our house beforehand as if packing for a visit—trying to remember socks, hair-combs, coats, money; Alexander sad and underprivileged as an orphan, Clarissa laced up in boots and bonnet. We move out of the door like ducks, half running down the path in front of the house towards the squat tower and the graves. This does not mean anything; a cold wind in a still sky and smell of the dark. Ghosts like bats hang in the entrance. In a roar of silence a man in a black suit steps sedately from my schooldays. Stone, dust, memory. A tinkle of laughter shut out by walls. Alexander in his thin coat staring into past and future. Clarissa an adolescent about to be touched by God. Rosalind with a handkerchief round her head like someone who works with her heart, her hands.

Matins in church goes so slowly that it seems to be moving backwards. The mouths of singers open and shut behind a note with the note in the air like chewing gum. There seems to be a hurricane against us making our flesh numb. The organist is deaf and lip-reads the vicar in a small mirror which swings. The vicar sways backwards and forwards to the mirror. There is a sort of panic, as if the boredom might send us mad. I think—What can I think about? Someone under torture; not knowing about prayer.

William would be starting off with Anna dressed in white. William had an old black car. Anna with one foot in the door like an advertisement for sweets. William's soft aristocratic face dissolving in a headwind. Scarfs and streamers behind it, a fast road by the edge of the sea.

Once when Rosalind and I had not long been married (my memory had to fill this gap in the church; this panic) our friends would drive up to our house on Sunday mornings and there would be this crunch of wheels on the gravel and a climbing out of a car with the doors open on each side like wings; lovers with sad furious faces and their girls behind dark glasses. People fell into love in those days as into a sort of pit, their arms up. Rosalind and I would wait for them on the lawn watching them as if they walked round the world in opposite directions. This was the middle time of love: when we had got what we wanted but it was a drug we could not stop.

In church attention wanders like a mouse beneath pews. Someone walks to the lectern: myself. A fine deep voice: not myself.

Sometimes in those days when we were first married I would play a vicarious role in the love affairs of our friends, sitting with one leg over the arm of a chair and blinking, picking a piece of wool off the leg of my trouser, listening to the stories that people told me of love and misery, of beauty and black light, of betrayal and adoring and despair. I was good at listening; a happily married man with my fine wise head and my background of crumbling walls and grey

64

stone buildings. Sometimes I would move slowly myself towards one of those cars parked on the gravel with their doors open each side like wings (power is evil, we have no excuses) and I would step in, closing the door, a girl on the seat beside me, a white dress and behind dark glasses. I would sit with my hands on the steering wheel and say— But what did you expect? The car with its bonnet, power, riding, the wheels cantering at corners. I would say—That's what life's like. We would drive to a hill where the wind blew, the flint and the rock and the birds screaming.

In the church I had been reading the lesson again. I could remember nothing of what I had been saying.

There was one particular friend of mine in those days (not long ago, five or six years, but a different world) who was called Angus MacSomething-or-other and who was important to me in that not only was he a great friend but he had a succession of girls that he brought to us moving in and out of the front seat of his two-seater car—girls with long bare arms and dark glasses and white dresses—girls which I would sometimes take over from him, temporarily, Angus MacSomething-or-other being exhausted with so much love. I remember this age with nostalgia because in fact it did not exist; I had known it before I was married but then from the inside, nothing true about it, but only afterwards when I was free making it a dream and thus desiring it: the dream of girls and men on mythical lawns and cars in sunlight. Angus MacSomething-or-other was a procureur for my imagination; I fell in love with these girls, the whole species of them with whom I had always been in love, but not now, with my wife Rosalind. I have always been and am only in love with my wife Rosalind.

But I fell in love with these girls for what they were not; for the dream, the unattainable. This is why most people fall in love; some sort of opposites in some ground in the unconscious. I remember then this crunch of gravel and the arrival of the car and the walk across the lawn; Angus MacSomething-or-other lonely as the man in the cigarette advertisement hitching up his trousers in the long and dusty street; myself ready to listen with one leg over the arm of a chair and blinking and picking at the sunlight. I listened to the stories which were always the same stories from the beginning of the world: once upon a time there were the sun and the summer trees and then transfiguration and then suicide.

The vicar leaned forwards and orated like the hanged man on the hook. One day someone would cut him loose and he would swing in the pulpit like a crane and be hurled into the furnace.

One day, I remembered, we went with Angus Mac-Something-or-other to a party at a huge house some twenty miles from Oxford; a party to be written up like disasters in the glossy magazines, men suspended in their dinner jackets and women stretched on steps like at Odessa. Angus this time had brought with him a big red-haired girl something quite new in racial memory; more powerful than usual, more wicked; having been driven from Oxford in Angus's fast car, herself a Ferrari. Angus had followed behind somewhere hitching up his cigarettes and lonely trousers. We were at this party on a lawn, by a marquee, in the bright summer darkness. Angus and his girl had been quarrelling all the way from Oxford; they were so much in love. I have to keep on saying this. He had hit her on the arm and bruised her. I remember this scene very well, the girl coming through the pillars and the dinner jackets and saying—Take me away—to me, which is what I had expected. I had one leg over a balustrade. How do we remember? Myself straightening my tie, my hair, going into that calm with the wind pulling me. Running behind it with all sails in the slipstream; the big red-haired girl ahead of me and me about to overtake her on the straight. Moving past the marquee lit with Chinese lanterns and going towards a lake, the road by the sea. Angus MacSomething-or-other standing behind on the shore. The scum and the scream of gulls. Lord Ullen's daughter.

We remember in envy, not regret; what we are now (in church, a row, a happy family) needing the past for its colour, tolerance. We know all this. The dangerous men are those with no memory; the ancient babies. Wisdom is a bit of cloth with the warp and woof breaking. The dust settling in the air; the people below choking.

Somewhere near the edge of the lake of this particular party there was an artificial grotto where in the eighteenth century tired business men had done black magic; as it were a club with cold buffet and the *Financial Times* in the corner, but nowadays done up with waxwork witches which people paid two-and-six to see on Sundays. For the night of the party this was lit with hellish cellophane to attract the guests; which it did not, there being too much of it outside with the smoke and the hideous wigs and harpies; except for the red-haired girl and I, who wanted somewhere to sit down, even the bench in front of the stewing pot of Miss Perkins the witch from Oldham. I mean this literally. We were in a grotto where people had once done black magic, and which now was on view as a party attraction. We read on a printed notice in front of the tableau of Miss Perkins that she had done things with pins and potions to people in the seventeenth century; until she had been caught, and split up the middle on an upturned axe. Such is love. Perhaps they had really tried to be sophisticated in those days, sitting round the board room table and ringing up for call-girls. I was cold, my arm round the waist of the big red-haired girl beside me, cutting the corners a bit, helped by the general air of filth and loneliness. I thought—We have our moments. There were a few other waxworks round the grotto, a hangman, a draw-and-quarterer or two, some victims with blood on their noses. I said to the big red-haired girl—You are in love? She said, rattling off like a funicular—I had heard this before. Funiculi Funicula. You don't do this because you like it, you do it because you have to. A moral position. I began embracing the big red-haired girl, a complex position like Rodin's kiss. The walls of the grotto seemed to be made of razors. I got a further grip on her and we began to float, sad steamers hooting, the bar and the wine-dark waves. This was the usual thing of course; when I say I talked to them of their life and loves I do not mean I talked to them of their life and loves. This is a universal disgust; a catastrophe.

I became aware of one waxwork in the grotto watching us as if it were alive. I must explain that Angus MacSome-thing-or-other had never before shown much interest in all this; he had not known about it, perhaps, yet he must have done; in the way we all lived vicariously in those days being both young and passionate. Perhaps it was useful to him to maintain his own lonely pain and his cigarettes. How else would he have been able to walk across the world like a cowboy with his trousers? But the waxwork who seemed to be alive did in fact now turn out to be Angus, who had followed us and was emanating in a corner in the grotto. His gaunt eyes stared at us. He was dressed as an executioner. I have forgotten to say that this was a fancy dress party, on the theme of Evil down the Ages—a subject coming into the height of fashion. I was dressed as a Sultan of Morocco; the red-haired girl was almost naked. Angus was appearing out of the shadows slowly; a medium's Red Indian contact. The big girl and myself had just climbed inside the Sultan of Morocco's burnouse; we were now struggling wildly to get out. I found myself facing Miss Perkins the witch from Oldham—a neat person like a Dicken's heroine. I could hear Angus behind me. I put on that smile that went through, and through the corridors of aristocratic buildings —old men stepping past wives and mistresses, past wives' lovers and the mistresses of lovers, doddering and intent and dreaming. I thought—Why should Angus mind? we all try for what we don't want: we get it regularly. I suddenly got a blow on the back of my head. I thought Angus must have taken off his leg and hit me with it. I have forgotten to say that Angus had a wooden leg, having lost his proper one at Cassino. I tripped over a bollard holding a rope and collapsed against Miss Perkins whose dress came off leaving her naked. Angus was shouting at the red-haired girl. He was carrying an axe, with which he seemed about to chop her. This particular Sultan of Morocco had been used to chop people's heads off. Whenever they wore yellow. I got between Angus and the girl and started talking to him. Perhaps it was all a joke: how terrible not to have a sense of humour! Angus had a black mask which stared at the ceiling. I looked up with it. He raised his axe as if to hit me again, so I pushed him, and he fell and this time his leg did come off: it wasn't wooden, but a steel thing with a knob on the end. He might now be able to hit me with it. I noticed a broomstick in a glass case on the wall, for protection. Angus had got up on one leg but he lost his balance and he reeled round the corner into another alcove. There he crashed against a Welsh virgin lying on her back on an altar with a loin cloth and one of her legs came off. I thought—This is absurd. Angus might push it up his trousers. We might both have a leg and fence with them. I was holding Angus's leg out to him like a fishing rod. Angus was lying on his back on top of the Welsh virgin. He seemed to be crying. The big red-haired girl was crying. Her mouth was bleeding. I had blood on the back of my burnous. We all began to shake. I remember this. All shaking. Wanting to be friends again.

We were standing up in church. I did not know how I had got there. I wondered if I might have been thinking aloud. Why did I remember this? There had been a blank; nothing had been happening. The organ was playing very slowly and there was a procession from the middle ages. Another few moments and then fresh air. What we were, what we had been. The last silence. Deluge. I thought— I want to die. We moved out of church, shuffling, cohorts of the defeated. By life, from the beginning. Rosalind and my children whom I adored. I thought—One day I will make sense of all this.

In the graveyard there was the bright sun and the men holding hats and the women laughing. In the valley the grey stone village quiet and English. A flag and music playing; a lump in the throat we would destroy. Oaks among hills and lawns, blue wind and far white sky. People lined up along the path. What does it mean; where is the connection? Down the gauntlet, tripping; our eyes tired.

Beyond the gate, up the path that leads towards our house, there was a solitary figure in a white shirt and grey flannel trousers. I recognised William. I thought—So she is not with him. I minded. I thought—We need the past like we need water. William was coming down the path to meet us. I thought—I am old, I feel nothing. William said "Church?" He had his face all screwed up. I said "Of course." There was too much sickness, nostalgia. I said "Church is so good for making you think about yourself." The crunch of gravel; the doors moving open at the sides like wings. I said "Everyone should think more of themselves." The path of the day stretching in front of us. What was there to look forward to, what should we do. I said to William "You're on your own?"

He had dropped back to talk to Rosalind. An English family out on this English summer day. Smart clothes on a dusty road. I must have walked ahead of them, looking for my roses, my paeonies, my dying forget-me-nots. What you did you worked at, being good with your hands. Life alone and beautiful.

Coming round the corner of our house by the rosebeds there was the edge of the drive where cars drew up on the gravel. Here William's car was parked with its doors closed like folded wings. To the right was another car, a Ford, with two people standing by it. Such as one sees in the desert. The light is reflected in heat, looking like water.

The soul is looking for water, being thirsty. The two people standing by this car were Charlie and Anna. Charlie looks like me from a distance. We have the same mannerisms, we copy one another. He and Anna were leaning over the bonnet, talking. The car was Charlie's car. The doors at the sides were open. Anna was wearing a white dress. Her hair was down and she wore dark glasses. I began copying Charlie, making an approach such as he might make, pointing at him and going half past him in parallel. Charlie put his head on his arms and started laughing. You walk straight past the person, on a sort of curve, as if the lines of the world moved away from one another. I clenched my fist and thumped it on the bonnet. It sounded sodden. I thrashed my hand up and down. Charlie said "I was just passing!" There was the whole day; a sort of ecstasy. I glanced at Anna and saw that gold skin and soft mouth and lovely eyes behind dark glasses. They might have been blind.

16.

"What are you writing now?" William said.

"A novel," Charlie said.

"Do you take your characters from real life or do you invent them?"

Charlie said "You take some things from real life, but you invent the story and all its connections and so on."

We were on the lawn outside the dining room. A marvellous day. All afternoon and evening.

"Why is it," William said, "that modern novels have to

be different, they can't just be stories of characters and action and society?"

Charlie said "We know too much about characters and actions and society."

William said "Then why write novels?"

We had had lunch. Earlier, when we had got back from church, we had stood on the gravel and had laughed with Charlie. Charlie had said he had just been passing. Anna had arrived earlier with William.

Charlie said "This is the point, we can now write about people knowing."

Anna was sitting some distance away making a daisy chain with Clarissa. As soon as she had arrived she had shown great interest in the children.

William said "I should have thought all that could be implied."

Charlie said "It is."

William said "I mean, the stuff about connections."

Charlie said "That's the realistic part."

William leaning on one elbow, picking at the grass. He had a way of stretching his jaw forwards as if something stuck in his throat.

Charlie said—"Suppose you were writing a novel about us now. What would you say?"

William looked round.

Charlie said "Here on the lawn. What are we up to?"

William said "I know what I'm up to."

"What?"

"Stephen and Rosalind invited me, with Anna."

"Oh yes" Charlie said.

"What are you?" William said.

73

Charlie was lying on his back. He had been stammering. I had suggested once that he write a novel about someone stammering.

William said "I suppose I'd just describe what each person's doing."

Charlie said "Rosalind's asleep. Stephen's weeding the garden. Anna's on the grass. We're having this conversation."

"That's what I'm saying," William said.

Charlie said "Rosalind's pregnant. Stephen's carrying on with this girl in Oxford. He's reached the age when he can't keep his hands off girls in Oxford."

Rosalind was lying on a garden chair with her feet up, her hands folded.

William said "What?"

Charlie said "He gets them out for the weekends. He has a guilt about it. So he makes up a story."

"What story?" William said.

Charlie said "This story."

Charlie had sat up. He began swatting flies. There weren't any flies.

"I'm not very clever," William said.

Charlie said "Shall we play tennis? There are millions of things happening in the world! People starving. Murdering. Seeing visions."

William said "I don't see about Stephen and the girls in Oxford."

Charlie shouted "Can you hear us?"

I shouted "Yes!"

Anna was putting a daisy chain round her neck.

Charlie said to William "What do you do in Oxford?"

74

William said "Politics and Philosophy."

Charlie said "People don't behave in the way we think they do. We know about all this."

We have a tennis court at the back of our house which is overhung by a mulberry tree. In autumn the mulberries fall and are squashed underfoot. The court is in a state of ruin: the net has holes in it and there were weeds in the grey gravel surface. The ball shoots or bounces vertically. William had white rubber shoes. Charlie played in bare feet. Anna's dress had a white skirt. William hit the ball hard as if cutting the top off it. Charlie played with Anna. I walked from side to side. There was a wind blowing some leaves. Charlie served and hit Anna in the small of the back. Rosalind sat on the side and watched. Charlie was trying to hit Anna. Charlie laughed. William whipped the ball over and it shot horizontally. The sun made us sweat. When I hit the ball it hung in the air like elastic. Charlie missed it and it bounced on the top of his head. Legs grew old; the body heavy. William slashed at us like nettles. Anna stood with her legs apart. I tried to see her. The sun in the square wall of garden. The mulberry tree.

I had tears in my eyes from so much laughing. I said "You will stay to dinner?"

Rosalind had gone. I looked for her by the apple trees. The delphiniums.

I was on my own in the afternoon.

I found her in the kitchen. Piles of saucers.

I said "Darling—"

"Yes?"

"I've asked them for tea. For dinner."

She had her back to me. White neck. Washing.

I said "I'll do it."

"Don't—"

"Don't what?"

"I'll do the dinner."

I wheeled a trolley on to the lawn with tea. People bending in profile above a jug. Bees among the irises. The milk cold as a well. Tomato sandwiches growing in the desert. One hand on the grass, a hole, a hip. The invasion again of summer. Anna with caverns. The grass with ants and beetles.

I said "Do you play tennis much at home?"

She said "A little, we haven't got a court."

"Where exactly do you live?"

"In southern Germany, but my mother spends part of the time in England."

"Your mother's English?"

"Yes. I was at school in England."

"Have you any brothers and sisters?"

"I have one younger sister."

"Is she beautiful?"

"Oh yes, very."

Anna's arms were of maize, olive. A cellar of husks. In southern Germany the baroque churches and little towns of matchsticks.

"Do you like it here?"

"Your house?"

"Oh no, Oxford."

William said "Come for a walk."

Anna said "I am so comfortable!"

I said "When we first came there was nothing, no garden, it had not been lived in for years. We had furniture for only two rooms. But we had to get out of Oxford."

"You don't like Oxford?"

"No."

William stood up and walked away.

"Why?"

I said nothing.

"Why do you work there then?"

I thought—I am fighting William.

I said "One has to."

Anna picked at the grass.

I said—"Come for a walk."

I stood up. She followed me. We walked along the apple trees. delphiniums. I said—We have a small paddock. She said—Do you ever keep a horse? No, it's not good riding. Through the huge grasses collapsing with milk. Parsley like scaffolding. Do you ride in Germany? No.

"Are you fond of William?"

"Why do you ask?"

"I wondered."

"Are there many dons like you?"

"Of course not."

Going on down the path. Ash. Pine trees.

"How lucky you are!"

"Why?"

"With your home. Your beautiful children."

I do not want anything. I have nothing to say.

"Partly luck."

"Oh what a view! How far can you see?"

In a clearing by a stile. A very young girl. One foot, the other behind. Arm raised. Pointing. Tossing her head about.

"I cut down these trees, I made the path up here last summer."

"How far does your land go?"

"This is the end."

I couldn't. Like clasping a cat. I could just look at her.

"It was so kind of you to ask me out here."

"I've loved it."

In the long grass. On the edge of the hill.

She said "Shall we go back?"

"Yes."

Walking in front of her the way we came. The delphiniums and the apple trees by the tennis court.

"You will stay for supper?"

She said nothing. I stopped. Hurt.

Her face troubled. Brown young face. Wide mouth.

"I would like to."

"But what?"

"I don't know about William."

"He'll stay. Why shouldn't he?"

She looked puzzled.

I said "I'll fix it." I thought—What do I want?

She went past me. Moving up the path. On the lawn there was Rosalind.

I sat down by Rosalind. I said "How are you feeling my love?"

I found myself miserable. Anna had gone into the house. There was nothing to do on Sundays. The long day.

Rosalind said "Are they staying?"

I said "I don't know."

I was sitting on the lawn, a body. A robot worked like a battleship.

"What's Charlie doing?"

I said "I'll see."

I went into the drawing room. There were bottles of beer on a tray. I drank. I shouted "Charlie!" The beer ran down in tunnels, caverns. Charlie came in from the passage He rubbed his hands.

He said "How are you getting on?"

I said "All right."

"What do you make of her?"

Standing close with beer, his one black tooth.

"I don't know."

"I agree!"

He wandered about looking out of the windows. His back to me. I said "Of course I know her quite well."

Charlie said "What does Rosalind think?"

I said "She groans."

"Groans!" Charlie looked amazed.

I did not know what we were talking about.

"What's this thing with William?" Charlie said.

"Well, he's after her."

"And how do you feel about that?"

I said "I don't feel anything."

Charlie said "Oh no." He stared into his beer.

I thought—Perhaps that was what he meant.

William put his head round the door. He said "Sorry."

"Come in, come in," Charlie said.

I thought—It's my house.

William said "Have you seen Anna?"

I said "I thought she was with you."

William said "No."

Charlie was pacing round the room.

I said "She was going to make you stay for supper."

"I think we ought to go," William said.

Charlie bounded out of the window and went across the lawn to Rosalind.

I said "It's all arranged."

I went through into the kitchen. To have something to do. Cold ham and salad. Potatoes. A woman came in each day to do the lunch and washing. Sunday a dead day. Objects. I stood and looked round the kitchen. Plastic and enamel. Began to get the plates out. Spaces. Filling them.

When I had walked with Anna down past the delphiniums and apple trees I could have spoken to her. I could have said—. In long grass on the hill. The world rushing.

I thought—I am making all this up.

Knives and glasses.

Taking in my hands, evil. That soft voice, cold eyes, risking everything. Like Rodin's figures in the palm of a hand. If you are dead enough you can do anything.

I had taken the plates and knives and forks and set them out in the dining room. William and Anna were on the lawn.

I thought—What in fact did I say? I made a path here last summer. Are you fond of William?

We know all about growing up. Changing.

I went back into the kitchen. I cut the ham. Another hour before supper. I would get drunk.

It might be better if we ruined ourselves.

I thought—Where are the children?

People nowadays prey upon their children.

I went to the window and called to Rosalind—"Where are the children?"

Rosalind said "Gone out to tea."

I said "I didn't know."

Anna said "Would it really be all right if we stayed?"

I said "You're going to stay?"

She was coming towards the window.

She said "If you're sure."

I thought—How marvellous!

The light behind her like Vermeer.

I said "Come and have a drink!"

The room with yellow curtains, black pelmet, blue wallpaper. There was now this still-life of flowers and a white statue. People stood in a doorway. The pale bubbles went up into the nose and mouth. We were all in the room, safe now.

William had his arrow in his eye from Hastings. Charlie and his blue-black chin. In the glass there was the genie with his pink and filmy eyebrow. It was still too tense; too dangerous. I wanted to be on my own.

I went out into the hall. A window to be mended. A bulb. Clean the piano.

Go in the garden and look in at them through the window. The sun so late at this time of year.

Could I remember what it was like to be in love.

Take the dog for a walk.

At the back of our house there is an old stable where the roof is falling in together with the tennis court and the paddock. There is an old rack where hay was once stuffed: tiles slip, showing the light through. These were once horses with heads tied to the bricks, the wooden manger. Munching. Watching out of the backs of their eyes. Men with short legs and thin straight backs hitting their legs, stroking.

We were all exorcised. Had no compulsion any more. I stood in the stable holding my drink. Ladies in long skirts and the springing steps of carriage wheels. We had lost all this.

At night the curtains and the doors of the dining room are closed so that for once it becomes a room with fragile chairs, rather Chinese, dangling. No longer walking down aristocratic corridors. I was sitting at the head of the table, wearing jeans, a loose shirt, rubber tennis shoes. Elegant red wine glasses. Soup. Rosalind must have made it.

Charlie and William were talking. I thought we had been through all this.

I said "But we're exorcised now, we don't have love or ambition any more. We're free. But we don't know what to do with it".

Charlie opened his mouth and tried to answer.

I said "If a person feels anything now we know why, it's his upbringing or digestion."

Charlie got a noise out like a hooter.

I said "It's like radioactivity, it kills. There's death, form, order. I'm not saying it's better or worse, it's just happening."

Charlie shouted "We know nothing!"

I said "Perhap's it's better."

The dining room table. Litter. Food scattered. Smoke and coffee. Miracles.

Charlie shouted "Let me speak!"

His stammer had got very bad. He seemed to be having a fit. It was short-circuiting him like electricity.

I poured out more wine.

"Oh God damn!" Charlie shouted.

82

I said "Of course, it's the same thing."

I was folding my tongue around my words. My tutorial voice. I seemed to hear it down a passage. I stopped. Looked at the plates. The grain of the table.

Charlie shouted "It's all so marvellous!"

William and Anna were whispering. They had been whispering on and off. Perhaps they had not been interested. Rosalind was listening to them. Rosalind had not been interested. A see-saw in my brain was going down one side. A negative discharge of electricity.

Rosalind said "Stephen, you tell them."

I said "Tell them what?"

"They want to drive back."

I said "Don't drive back."

William said "It's after eleven."

I said "You can climb in somewhere."

I thought they must think I was drunk. I couldn't get my consonants round my vowels.

Charlie said "What time do you have to be in?"

William said "Eleven."

Anna said "I'll drive."

Charlie said "You havn't got a license."

Anna said "William, can I drive, I'd love to drive your car!'

Rosalind said "Oh do stay."

I said "Why can't William drive?"

I had my head to one side. Flames. Charcoal.

William said "They think I'm drunk."

I said "What have we had? Three bottles!"

Anna said "Let's stay."

I said "I'll drive."

Rosalind said "No you won't."

I said "Charlie can drive."

Charlie said nothing.

I said to Rosalind "You drive!" I wanted to laugh.

Rosalind said to William "You can get in just as easily in the morning."

William had stood and held Anna by the arm. Charlie was looking at Anna.

I said to Anna "Can you get in in the morning?"

Anna said "Yes."

William said "Come on."

I said "William, you'd better stay."

William said "Why do you want us to stay?"

I said "There've been all these crashes."

His face had gone lopsided. Hurt.

Rosalind said "I'll make up the beds."

I said to William "You are a bit drunk."

William said "Are you?"

My face had gone so stiff I could not move it. My voice from the far end of a passage.

Rosalind had gone out. I got up and walked out into the hall. To put my head under the tap. The dog came at me sideways like a jelly. I sometimes wanted to kick the dog. I was in the hall by the telephone. I thought—I am sitting by the telephone: I have heard some terrible news. I couldn't think why I had come here. Rosalind was making up the beds. How many? A joke. William was jealous. I could go to Anna's room and I could say—.

I went back quickly into the dining room.

Charlie was alone.

I said "What's happening?"

Charlie said "They're staying."

I wondered which room Anna was in. There was the spare room, one we called my dressing room, and a bed at the back by the kitchen.

Charlie said "How's your book going?"

I said "Oh all right."

"What's it about?"

I said "The usual."

Charlie said "Which room is anyone going to?"

His face had fallen sideways. Shining. A blue-black moon.

I shouted "It's a farce!"

We laughed.

The others all seemed to have gone to bed.

There was once a time at weekends in country houses (I had thought this before) when figures came out of their rooms and moved about the passages like ghosts passing through one another, holding lamps or white nightdresses and slippers, lovers and mistresses and the mistresses of lovers. Fertility rites with bats in caves and birds whooping in the tall trees. Husbands and wives walking around with withered knees, going to bed or fetching things from the bathroom. A racial memory. I found myself alone in the dining room having dropped off to sleep. These were bones and feathers, blood, chairs set for predatory ancestors. Someone might return. I began to tidy. It was the dead time, near midnight.

I had gone into the hall and was at the foot of the stairs looking up when I saw Rosalind at the top of the stairs in a dressing-gown. At least I thought it was Rosalind. She seemed about to come down. When she saw me she stopped. I was thinking about other things; about Anna. Going up the stairs I passed her without looking. I was sad: husbands behave badly when they are drunk. I went across the landing. I thought—We can make it up in the morning.

When I got to our room there was someone in bed. I thought—But she has come here! Then, arriving closer, I saw that the person in bed was Rosalind. The lights were on. I sat on the edge of the bed. She was asleep. I thought— We have to be very careful. The room with the furniture waited for the lights to go out. I thought—The person at the top of the stairs must have been Anna. She had been wearing Rosalind's dressing-gown. But she had not been wearing Rosalind's dressing-gown. She had seemed to be much darker. There was something undecided and crucial about this. All the things coming out after midnight. This is what I had meant. Now we were at the mercy of things; not deluded.

V

17.

ON television there is a programme called *Conversation Piece* in which people sit at various levels as if posing for a painter. They carry on an informal conversation having been rehearsed carefully according to angles, subjects, timings. Many of them are people I have known at some time in my life. As a face comes up I remember something vindictive about it; a ruined marriage, drink, homosexuality. This is the programme on which Tommy Parker appears in his black roll-neck sweater. A boy from Chatham weeping in my room. They talk and give their views on art, politics, morals. The words flick out like tongues of lizards. To eat, paralyse. Then going into their stomachs again. I am envious of these people: not having been asked to do it myself.

Towards the end of this summer term my wife Rosalind went away to stay with her mother; being pregnant and having to look after the large house. She took our daughter Clarissa with her. For a time our son Alexander stayed behind and I took him each day to school; then he too went, with ear-ache, and the house was empty. Our daily help came in each day and cooked me breakfast and left supper. I watched the television. I found myself not wanting to work in the garden.

There is a laboratory in Oxford where a human brain is kept alive. It is in a wooden cabinet like an old frigidaire. I was taken to see it during these days and I wanted to ask questions about it—does it feel, think. Men in white coats worked round it with tubes and wire. I found I could not ask my questions. Out of respect. Or perhaps fear. I was on the edge of a little group of people.

Once during these days I went to spend the day with William at his parent's house in the country. William had invited me weeks ago, before the day he had spent at Palling. William lived in another of those huge stone houses which people paid two-and-six to see on Sundays. When I arrived they were already there, the sightseers, behind a barbed wire and a baroque balustrade. They seemed to be at the scene of some disaster. The friends of the family were separate from them in a small courtyard with creepers and striped chairs. In a compound.

When you are too much on your own you have a feeling of profusion, of intensity. I had become obsessed with this split between our public face and our private helplessness. The men on television. The brain in the Oxford frigidaire.

When I arrived at William's house (Rosalind had been gone for a week now) the people in the courtyard began to regroup in a protective way against the stranger: a chromosome formed of things that were not alive but which acted as if they were: the group, aristocrats. A survival of the fittest. The men had small heads and hands; the girls were smooth-bottomed cylinders with little taps and dials at the top. Watching William I saw how he still had some separate identity from them; but soon would not. Going back to foeti, centuries away from their knees.

Anna was not there. I had been expecting Anna. Beyond the fence were the crowds who reproduced themselves by division, like primitive cells.

In the evening, after the sightseers had gone leaving the grass dead and brown, we played a game, a sort of house game, the men, all ten of us—going through to a neutral part of the house between the main block and the servants'—a long stone corridor with high windows and cream panelling. There were family portraits on a wall—men in full armour and wigs, fleshy faces like women, a few recent ones dry as matchsticks. The game was a sort of football that the men had played at school; they had all been to the same school, of course, they were at home in the huge corridor. They took off their coats and smoked their last cigarettes. There was a green baize door at one end and at the other an archway like a cloister. I was the only one who did not know the game; had not been to their school, of course, and of a different century. I could hardly remember this. Pudding, marmalade, grease on the table. I did not know why I had wanted to come. The game was played with an old toy, a relic of the nursery, a sewn up thing like a donkey. The men tucked their trousers into their socks. Above us were the portraits of plumes and horses and shining metal. I was sent to the far end to keep goal; in my twill trousers and spotted bow tie. Beyond me gothic vaulting like a church. Arms holding candelabra. The game was a scrum along one wall: a boy held the ball to his middle and was lifted off his feet as in a mock-up of birth, a communal buggery. The portrait above me was of William's grandfather who had been killed at Mons. All brown, badly painted, with flat eyes and upturned moustache. They could not paint in those days because they had no depth; they had wanted to die. Further on was an ancestor who might have fought at Blenheim: he had a breastplate and a long black wig. The girls of the house-party had come to one end of the corridor and were looking in like Americans at a village tea party. The scrum was a sort of bowel with a gut gone. William's grandfather had fought in the mud with his deerstalker hat and sporting rifle. They had all wanted to die being so beautiful, so immortal. In the ice and the just visible noses.

I saw emerging from the scrum headfirst a struggling thing, a turd, trapped painfully at the waist. A boy with the ball held close to him. They were trying to push him back inside. Freud had something about all this: aristocrats: only good for fighting. The boy with the ball was William: his face like bruised roses. He came at me suddenly, having kicked himself free. You trod on them with your hands up. I realised I was the only one between William and the door. The door was the goal. I have to explain these things. I was standing with legs braced against the rush of plumes and lances. A squat man in homespun. William charged me like a battering ram in the stomach. I was carried along a little way on the back of his neck; a wave of water, pain, a picador's horse. My long mane floating. I thought at this moment—I understand now this thing about William and his ancestors; their necks are on the hard ground and their horses in the saddle; the two lines meeting in a sort of crotch, an ecstasy. I was carried along with my small fists in William's back. Then came the cavalry, the hordes, the men with choppers. We all had to get our heads down into the position of the English public schoolboy. As de Sade would say. At this moment of pain we are not accustomed, not brought up to war, rather disliking it. A knife in the back better than these wigs and khaki. I caught a glimpse again of the old queen from Blenheim with his long black hair. I was in the middle of the scrum, my feet off the ground, myself beginning to kick. Someone jumped on me. I must explain that these were grown men, nineteen and twenty. They all wanted to die: adolescents in mud and grey barbed wire. The person on top of me had his arm around my throat. I wanted to wave my handkerchief—to say—to make this clear—You do this because you're bored, you do this because you're frightened. Or was this too simple? I burrowed into the scrum to take the weight off. One of the faces in front of me was William's. I put my hand on the back of William's neck. Behind the barricades and the paving stones. By squeezing on William's neck I could hurt him. Generations of Williams straining, shitting. To softly bite him. Someone behind me twisted my ear: I began really to fight, with my knees and elbows. Like we did it at home. You can hear the birds. I worked my knee up so that it was under William's face. His teeth bared. I brought my knee up into William's face. I saw now what happened. It was a mercy to kill them. To put them out of their misery.

I had a letter from Charlie.
Dear Stephen,
    Thank you for putting us up the other day. You and Rosalind are a sort of touchstone in my life. I don't know what I'd do without you.
    I was in London the other day talking to some tele-

vision people and I mentioned you as someone who might do for them on Conversation Piece. Would you like this? If so, get in touch with them.

Here's the name and number.

I have tried to explain all this. I want to say—this is the letter from Charlie, this the football game with William. There were other things at this time—driving in and out of Oxford, my pupils, the common room; going for walks under the willows by the river. But I have to say— This and that have a meaning.

There is this letter now on my desk from Charlie. Or it might be from Stephen. The writing is old, slightly faded. How many years? I told him I would not write the story for three years. Where are we now? William is dead. Anna I don't know. I wonder what has happened?

She was on the bank by the upturned car. On the bed in our spare room. I was pleased by the letter from Charlie. I thought I would visit the television people. What else was there? Of course, you can't prove anything. It is all just chance. We want to think this. Sleepwalking.

A building slightly peeling with a wedding-cake facade; inside a lift, a man in a peaked cap, a concertina gate, the old man chewing, the lift with brass buttons. On the third floor an office with scrubbed wood and secretaries. A pile carpet and lights with small holes; a copper head with a white face, a daffodil buried all summer. I said—I have an appointment with Mr. Rounceval. Pale silver lips, smooth cheeks, black eyebrows.

On a contemporary table magazines with pictures of dead

girls. Will you wait please. In this tomb an ancient Juliet. Armless sofa, smell, heat. High heels seen from the back when you are old. *Queen, Newsweek, Films and Filming.* Those thin soft arms and flames from the faggots. A trade magazine with photographs of my friends from *Conversation Piece.* Tommy Parker with his crew-cut through coloured mica.

The secretary returned all in one piece, a wheel, that new invention. Mr. Rounceval, Mr. Rounceval, Mr. Savile. That will do then. Copper coloured hair, small eyes, below them nothing. A prisoner's fingers against barred windows. I rose to follow. Outside the earth, the air, violence coming down like parachutes. We walked across the carpet, a man in striped trousers, thumbs in waistcoat, blind and brilliant. Balloons filled with water. Intestines of power. The unfledged eggs.

A cubicle of cream and plywood rough at the edges. The old moulding of what had once been a house now broken and melted. A voice in the next cubicle talked and shouted. Police. Fire. A pale narrow desk. Mr. Savile was a short dark man in a cardigan. We must rally round Savile. I recognised him as a boy from my minor public school. He had done something in the observatory. People were always doing things in the observatory. To see better with. A telescope and two brass cogwheels. Savile said "Bill Rounceval is ill." He looked ill himself. He came round his desk like the man in the western film. Hips round his knees. I could not remember what exactly he had done in the observatory "He's lying all alone in bed in St. Thomas's" Savile said. "I'm so sorry" I said. "I've got to go and see him" Savile said. He stood by the desk. On that dusty street, that hand on holster, verandah and wooden pillars. Something to do with a boy called Eccleston, the school tart. Flight Lieutenant Eccleston, A.D.C. to someone. "I don't really know him" I said. "Don't know Bill Rounceval?" Savile said. He looked annoyed. He had a yellow skin, an electric razor, tufts at the top of his cheeks which at school had been called buggers' grips. "You're Stephen Jervis aren't you?" I said "Yes." Another secretary tapped away in a corner: the only thing man was good at; the Post Office, the telephone. Savile said "What did Bill Rounceval want you for?" His secretary bent down in front of a filing cabinet; a behind in the bar of the western saloon. A tinkling piano. Savile watched the secretary. I said "I had an appointment with him." The secretary came up with a file. Her yellow fingers. Savile said "Do you ever see Francesca?" I couldn't remember about Francesca. Savile with the cowboy expression. There had been a time when we had all been in a car, in the front seats. Charlie had hit his head against a lamp post. I said "Francesca!" I remembered—the Provost's daughter. I said "How is Francesca?" Savile was looking through the file. I caught the eye of the secretary, who wore a mauve cardigan. I said "Of course I remember." Those mauve eyelids, hard skin, helmets of copper. Savile said "Of Palling Manor, Palling?" I said "Yes." He said "Bill was thinking of you for *Conversation Piece?*" A distraught man like a jockey suddenly came in. He said "Where's Bill?" Savile said "He's in St. Thomas's Hospital." The man like a jockey sat down: he seemed on the point of collapse. Francesca had her eyes closed running, running. We had laughed so much in those days. The man like a jockey said "I didn't know he was ill." Savile said "He's very bad." The telephone began ringing. The secretary picked it up. The three of us sat at the far end of the cubicle. We had been on some party. I said "I think he was thinking of me." The man like a jockey said "He was all right the day before." Savile watched the secretary. The secretary put her hand over the mouthpiece. I thought—Now let me get out: let the world take over to my salvation. The man like a jockey mopped his forehead. I said to Savile "Never mind." Savile said "I don't know what his plans were." The man like a jockey said "Jesus Christ." I thought—we are being experimented with; people are watching us with cameras and microphones. Savile said "Perhaps I could let you know." Outside the pyre was being piled up with faggots. My legs felt heavy; my head a balloon. I said to Savile "I must go." He said "Why don't you come along and see Bill Rounceval?" He was talking to the man like a jockey. This was an office in a television building. I said "Goodbye." Savile said "Give my love to Francesca." I said "I haven't seen Francesca." They must have something else to say to me. The man like a jockey was shaking. Savile was trying to catch the secretary's eye. The secretary was sitting in front of a typewriter. I left them.

What I remember about Francesca was my own propensity to tears; I would cry for exercise, for the world, a sort of madonna. Francesca was the Provost of St. Mark's daughter. I had loved her once; or had said I did. I had known her in another world. We did not like the truth: we did not know it. I found her number in a telephone book.

This was the afternoon of the second day of my visit to London. In the morning I had been to the television office. At lunch I had seen a film. I went into the telephone, out of it. I was in an underground station of white tiles. Francesca's name had been put into my head by Savile. Savile was standing in for Rounceval, who was ill. Rounceval's name had been given to me by Charlie. There was a small square mirror showing my tie. The crowds in the station were like corn.

I had come to London for two days, taking time off from the summer term. Rosalind and the children were in the country.

I remember crying with Francesca in the front seats of cars. All my early life had seemed to happen in the front seats of cars. For security. So that you could always move on; not be caught anywhere.

I went into the telephone box. The speck of dust in London. The brain in the Oxford frigidaire. It dropped on the white tiles, splashing.

I rang Francesca. I hoped Francesca wouldn't answer. She did. I said "Francesca?" To prove the independence of the will. "This is—" My name. A betrayal. You toss a penny: murder a pawnbroker. How else to prove the will? I said— "I just wondered—" I asked her out to dinner. Francesca had never understood why I cried. You do what you don't want. It had seemed I was not happy. I said "You can? That's marvellous!" I wished I had not rung her.

When I was out of the call box I was pleased I had asked her to dinner. Now my two days in London would have some point. This is what people did. Francesca had once been my mistress. I would meet her and we would talk about old times. I would stay late. We would go to bed together. London was so beautiful, so much light about it. Sexuality in the skin and the mind. I had some time to wait before dinner. I was moving through streets hoping for excitement around some corner. Having exerted the will. I could fall down on the pavement and say—I am ill, dying. To compose myself. For that tragic time when I was twenty three, a beetle with its legs in the air; someone turning me over and putting a foot on my body, my eyes. I was growing young again. Something to hold on to with my claws. Grown brittle now. The streets of London so beautiful. Faces dreaming on corners. No one alive now. With their teeth and talons: the swordfish bill.

I met Francesca at her flat. Without flowers, without a personality, having disposed of it along the route. A package in a litter bin. Francesca was a middle-aged matron with her teeth going. I had not remembered this. I wanted to run. I had got my foot in at the door. No one wants to do this, you do it for a living. Have pity. I embraced Francesca. She had one of those rooms I had forgotten, with paperbacks and a divan and a record player. Perhaps I could still do this: there are rules. How to use a person for your own advantage as an object. The ultimate sin. Francesca was like a Spanish lady at a bull-fight, all lace and garters. When she smiled we were terrified: I was a hairy thing with arms and legs. I wanted to sleep. Perhaps this was charm, the art of seduction. The more you try the less you hope for. Or the statistical technique, the more you try you exhaust the numbers. Francesca and I were talking from two corners of the ceiling. How long is it since. What have you been doing. Perhaps she would faint: then I could go home. It was only an hour and a half to Palling. She said—How marvellous to see you! In order to catch a spider you put a piece of paper on the floor, the spider turns away, you put the paper back again, it turns away, you get two pieces of paper. My knees stretched out of perspective. Francesca was a music-hall heroine. You become tethered to this, made a god of it. The age of religion.

I tried to concentrate on Francesca. We were in the sitting room of her flat, making conversation. I had not seen her for five or six years. We had once been in love. I had now rung her up to ask her out to dinner. My wife Rosalind and the children were away in the country.

We were talking of old friends. What had happened to so and so. I was holding a drink.

It would take two or three hours.

There is a love scene in which the same thing is done repeatedly: a head against a neck, turning, the long hair falling. Francesca was thirty-five now. Her hair was going stiff. People have nothing to say from beyond the grave, when they try to make contact with one another. It is a beautiful day up here: it is going to be all right. Swinging around the moon. Francesca and I were exchanging goods in a curb-side deal. We had no capital. We should start weeping like we used to do. No wonder people do it. Carried out paralysed, kings or gods in electric chairs.

We had come to some pause in our conversation. We were drinking to hurt the brain: a grating through which water flowed. If enough poison came down like weeds then there would be peace, tension. I thought—Tomorrow I will see the dam collapsed; the muddy swirl.

Up till now I had not listened. In this room, dark-haired, soft, no one listened. She had slight hollows in her cheeks which at an angle made her beautiful. I thought—I only want something. She said "And how are your child-

98

ren?" I told some story about Alexander. She smiled. "How sweet!" There was some justification of religion: it recognised only an abstract hope. I said "And how have you been?" Her nose, her soft upper lip, padding like pain. I had been thinking something of importance. Not about need, contact. Francesca went on about some holiday in Spain. Why didn't I say—It is no use. A short story: a scene in a film. I began to tell Francesca about some holiday in Spain. If you did get contact then what would you do? Scream with hand in front of the face. Running.

Francesca and I were discussing where to have dinner. There was a blank place at a crossroads on a windy night. I said "Let's get drunk!" That sleeping thing in the car; a sea-cow being prodded to sensibility. Francesca laughed. I said "That's a lovely dress!" She looked amazed. I thought —Why shouldn't I say That's a lovely dress? I had almost lost myself now, a parent shouting among a field of daffodils. Two of us, hand in hand, out in the street. Two children. Francesca tossed her head. How do you act love? A hop and skip; a murmur. And then the scene with the long and falling hair, repeatedly. Everyone looks up and says—They are in love. They are on their own. Where do these myths come from, the liver, the heart. I wanted to cut them out so they would be on their own. I would then be free. I would watch them poison the ground. Mutation. Hormones. In a hundred years there would be nothing.

Francesca and I went to an expensive restaurant. It was pink. All these things we know now. I stared into her eyes. She began to tell me the story of her life. She worked in consumer research. You came across interesting people in consumer research. I decomposed. The wind blew through the walls and body. How to break up bourgeois society. I thought—Now it will be all right. The fields flat, the footprints in winter. A man in the back streets killing. Francesca was talking of her boss. A good man. The buildings like skyscrapers falling round the knees. Above them the pale body of nothingness. I touched Francesca's legs with mine under the table. There was white soup, bread, chicken, mushrooms, spinach. I said "How extraordinary!" I was stretching out around the room, raising my head as the water came up to my eyes. In the corner a young man lurked: a cuckold with his finger on the button. They had pigs' eyes. Human anatomy is similar to pigs'. Is impossible any more to fight against killing.

We lacked a Viennese count with a violin. We were on to our second bottle. This evening was going very well, a man of ninety and a teenage model. The food settled down and you lay on top of it. I began talking of the world; an age of decadence, the divorce of love from power. I had to use my charm, my eccentricity. A cloud was moving over the downs. There was the thing in the corner with the cigarette, the soft mouth. The bridge with the ice-flows in the river. The inner division and the outer state of the world. Symbolic. The skyscrapers with their skirts falling. The man chewing. There was no more space; the food like coal over green fields. Mist, rain, wine; darkness like phosphorus. For every good action there had to be the appalling war. I could not think of the answer to this.

Francesca and I were getting ready to leave the restaurant. There were some actresses with red hair in a corner. I said "Let's go somewhere else." Francesca said "Where?" To Marrakesh. Timbuctoo. Camels like skeletons. Turrets. We turned into the street. Radioactivity; the lost direction. We were going the wrong way into the hills. Things stretched their necks out. Dying. Laying their eggs away from the sea.

Under my hand there was a piece of bone and muscle, Francesca's arm covered with cloth. Something trotted on the sand in front of palm trees. The shrill cries of birds and hunters. At the corner of the street there were newspapers and the hot wind from the poles. The balance of life lay between infinitesimal temperatures: I said "Let's go home." Now we were mourners at a funeral. In black, heads down, from the tops of our eyes seeing the visitor. Francesca made no objection. You live in the present, which does not exist: it exists in memory. Those old men with their teeth gone and their hair out, shaking. The future hitting you like a wave in the back. It was so cold. I held Francesca's hand in a taxi. We were going back to the old life with the sun and snow and children with muffs round their ears. Reindeer. I started to kiss Francesca. Mouth coming up to the worm, the hook. A mother's face. Grey fish's lips and jerked up through the palate. Francesca was soft, warm, a sleep, an exercise. Floating above my head the starry world.

We were now two people in front of a doorway. Francesca was looking for a key. I was dressed in an overcoat. The street was empty. I looked this way and that past the dustbins. To make sure. Hurry or you may get caught. Francesca had long legs and thin ankles. I was a shadow against the wall, blown by that wind. Take enough trouble and you can destroy anything. My brain poisoned. That marvellous softness.

There is now going to be a celebration, dance, beat-up, pas-de-deux on the gramophone. The black man on a dark night in the coal cellar. Toot toot di toot. A non-existence with dark hair and wooden faces. Francesca and I were back in the bed-sitting room, bathroom. After how many hours. There was a bedspread made of dust. I had been to sleep and woken up again in a thousand years. What was it I had wanted? A gothic castle, dream, terror. Francesca went into the bathroom. I sat on the bed at right angles with my feet up. Now at this quiet time: heroically I lit a small cigar. Now I could be that person with sideburns and the long, tapering carrots. You push him and he grows—a tufted cowboy. Somewhere a bird was fluttering at the window. You shot it. A mutation was taking place in the deep and wandering world. Francesca came up to the bed. Now drop your hands with the flags and banners. The mechanic has his spanner and oil. You have bright fingers. Don't move, move, or it will break. The body full of lights. Light. The love of machine.

Francesca wore a black woollen dress. Hairspray, mascara, lipstick. In several flavours with cream. Her hair grew from pores like a snowfield. Across the snow there was a building with the blank wall of the mind. Leaning over the landscape I was myself a cloud, a hand on her breast, a nerve in my cheek twitching. That beauty of earth, sky, iris, pupil. Behind me there was a row of windows and a chimney smoking. The power house. We had discovered everything, youth, memories. I began to walk across the cold harsh landscape. Bump: the look of the dog. The cow with its front legs like flippers. A turtle. Now I was in this white light, cave. I saw a bird on the curtain rail. I was in Francesca's room. The bird's bright eye was watching me. I was holding on to the body, the loved one, the child in pain. Achilles with his sword knelt over the body of his dead hero. Go into the darkness again. This sickness of mind will die soon: the molecules, atoms, rubbing. There are gyrations that do not belong to me: an eccentric with pistons and gears. The windows are high up in the long wall of the power house. Platforms and rails and iron stairs. There is so much noise: on this bed a murder might be committed. A child in a blanket. Dirt coruscating. If I could cry, kick it; ride the earthquake. I am so pleased to be here again.

You do not think this has anything to do with you. You are working through a thick glass with pincers. At the end of your long fingers there is a piece of radioactive material. You lower it into its protective sheath. Your arms are stretched out as part of your personality beyond the glass wall. A tool is a limb. The white root is the long stem of the flower. The flower is of gold petals. The metal changes. Nothing of this is seen. It is all known by its effect. A fish with its wings out breathes air, fire. It is known from the inside. Its eyes are white and invisible. It glows; spreading outwards. The man manipulates. The man is dead.

Now I remember this I am so happy, rolling on that old sail, tethered. If we are brave enough we hold the sea: a race of gods and horses. We forget but this time will remember. Smile again. Please. I do so adore being with you. The muscle from the back. Within layers of lead. The mysterious explosion.

We are all gone. One mistake and the world is over.

I am like a child, crying. Some soft throat and there is no noise. Such a small one. Into the cold air, I will not live. An arm, body. On another arm, body. That pattern of

103

pain with palms to the ground. A body of bronze. Thing of beauty.

I opened an eye. The curtains on which there had once been a bird had now gone. I was in a room, pink, with the light shaded. The point of humanity. I began to remember something else that I had not wanted. There was a patchwork quilt. Her head was turned away. It is reason that distinguishes man from the beasts. They are so beautiful with their great teeth and sleepy eyes. Francesca had brown skin. The vultures waited. The wrinkled skin so soft, so beautiful. We would smoke a cigarette, tap out time till hunger came again. One day it would. I sat up and put my arm around my knees. There was the pink light on a dressing table. Francesca was so young, I would always remember her. The soul flies away and becomes a bird on a curtain on a fresco.

Francesca stretched her arms up. Her muscles and breasts. The wounded after battle are in long lines between archways. The general walks up and down: a nurse follows. A finger, a thumb, stroking down mascara. Soot from gunshot. The cold cerebral eye. Distant; dispassionate. I do not want to remember.

The body is so beautiful that we mourn over. Love and death, a cup of tea, the brain again. Francesca pulled her clothes towards her. I was in a room with a pink lampshade. I had made love to Francesca. You are in an empty room with clothes, bedclothes, divan, gramophone. There is someone dressing. You are so pleased. You want to be away again.

I was that smooth thing with the waistcoat and trousers. Making the world go round. I am this boy on the corner with his knife, my feet on the floor, my finger on my shirt buttons. That lonely thing with my hair swept back, the blank wall and high windows. I said "Francesca darling." The words came out. There was painted furniture, sweetness, shadow. Her long and lovely back. This had happened. We make a god of it. Defeat. I am almost gutted. Let me become that thing, empty, floating past the walls of crumbling buildings. No more a person. Quick. Let me remember it.

When I got home, travelling very late that night or rather in the early morning, passing on the empty road that place at which I never quite determined where I became the different person, the person that I am at home; there, by the stone lions, the gravel crunching, I found the dark facade of my house, my ghost, with nothing in it alight, the door locked. I was tired and rather drunk. I went round the side of the house with no pause, sleepwalking. A clown rolling and spinning slightly. To a window at the back. I had done this before in the old days, lacking a wife in curlers and with a rolling pin. I went through the window headfirst and fell on the floor of a lavatory. There was never a lock on this window: this window never had a lock. In the corner I was a bag of bones on the lino. I had to get to bed. How uncomfortable was this prison! My jaw sagged. I crawled to a light and switched it. My eyes blazed. In the hall there were rows and rows of chairs. I sat down. I had been away for centuries. We are judged by facts, not feelings. A jury of furniture. There were footsteps on the landing.

There was no one else in the house. Rosalind and the children were still away. The woman who came in each day left at tea time. A tramp. A murderer. You grasp the poker by the handle. You bash him. I sat with my mouth open.

A light came on upstairs.

One foot in no man's land.

I wiped my face. Drew a breath. Was glad of company.

I went to the bottom of the stairs and looked up. Upside down, above me, there was a face just like my own.

I put a hand to my heart.

Charlie.

I was pleased to see Charlie. I thought I was going to be sick. The clown with the long pole and the tea tray. Charlie came down and sat on the stairs. I went half way to meet him. I said "I've been to London." The carpet on the stairs wanted patching. Rails with brass knobs. Charlie seemed to have nothing on under a dressing gown. I said "I saw the television people." Charlie had been here a week ago with William and Anna. They had spent the night and then had gone in the early morning. I said "And Francesca, do you remember Francesca?" Charlie said "How is Francesca?" I said "She's very well." Charlie had taken out a pipe and was blowing through it. I said "I don't understand what one wants." I thought about this. I said "You think you want it then you don't." Charlie banged at his pipe. I said "St. Augustine was wrong." Charlie said "St. Augustine?" I said "He said that in sex there was no reason, will: but the trouble is there's too much." I didn't know what Charlie was doing here. I said "You do it as a sort of discipline; an exercise."

Anna had appeared on the landing above me. She was wearing black trousers and a yellow sweater. I said "Have you been here all the time?" She had her hair done up with the sides brushed back. I said "We're talking about sex."

I began to hear myself saying this, gradually. I said "The way how to spread confusion." Anna was blushing. Or perhaps drunk; rather red and puffy. I said "Let's have some food." I went through to the kitchen. I wondered how long Charlie and Anna had been here. One place had been laid in the kitchen for breakfast. I went back to the hall. I saw Charlie and Anna whispering. They were always whispering. Or Anna and William. I said "I'm going to make an omelette." Charlie said "We'll come and watch you." Back in the kitchen there were cupboards, shelves, drawers. Men in white coats round the frigidaire. I said "How long—" A light went up showing eggs, butter, milk. Anna and Charlie were standing behind me. Charlie said "We don't want anything." I listened to the frigidaire. It was cold. I said "Rosalind's been away nearly a week." Charlie said "How is Rosalind?" I said "Very well." I thought I should put my hands on Anna's shoulders and stare into her eyes. Francesca was still on my face, my hands. A breath like pollen. I put on some water to boil. They were sitting round a table with a red plastic top. I wished they would talk. I was tired. I was longing not to go to bed.

Charlie said "We couldn't keep away." I said "I'm flattered." Anna came round to the stove and said "Shall I cook?" I said "Can you cook?" Anna said "At home I cook for my family." Charlie said "What do they cook, Jews?" I began to laugh. I felt dreadfully embarrassed. I went to see if the water was boiling. The surface was grey with silver bubbles at one side. I thought—The brain will take anything. I said "Eggs." Anna looked as if she had been crying. Charlie was holding her and had put his head on her shoulder. I said "If you live too much on your own you get a little mad." Charlie seemed to be taking a bite out of her neck. I heated the frying pan. I said "Don't you want any supper?" They were like Venus and her dark brown Bacchus, Charlie said "Her grandfather sold a hundred thousand Austrian Jews." Anna said "That's not true." Charlie said "I'm not saying it's right or wrong, I'm saying it happened." I beat the eggs up. There were bits of black stuff in them like chickens. Francesca's room had had a pale pink lampshade. I had sat on the edge of the bed with my buttons. Charlie said "He used to flog his serfs in the market square." Anna said "Why do you say all this?" I thought—I must remember, the three of us, the stove, the cupboards. Charlie said "That's why they wear those leather trousers in Austria, to get a bit of air round their balls." Anna said "We heard you." My hands were moving slightly off centre above the frying pan, a wheel gone wonky. I wondered if we could all sleep together. Charlie and me and Anna. Like people in California. Or soldiers in the Crimean war. I had a plate, a scraper. The smell of butter. Yellow fingers of egg. Charlie's face appeared close beside me suddenly. He said "Can we really stay here?" I said "I thought you were." Charlie's face went away. He began hitting his pockets. He said to Anna "Can you get my cigarettes?" Anna ignored him. I flipped my omelette on to a plate. Charlie said "You thought we'd been here since last week?" I said "At least." Charlie's face came close again. He said in a loud whisper "It wasn't me." I thought—I must get out of this. I walked round the table, linoleum, patches in squares. Anna was sitting. I said in a strange voice "Grub's up!" I walked back to the stove going up and down at one side like a man with a wooden leg. Charlie began eating the omelette. Anna

said "I thought you didn't want any." Charlie said "I didn't."
I was making tea, the white inside of the electric kettle.
Anna said "Then why are you eating it?" Charlie shouted
"God damn!" He pushed his plate away. I thought—I must
be nice to them: they need it. I said to Anna "Where are you
sleeping?" She was a prim girl, round, Dutch. I said "I
don't mean anything!" I began laughing. Anna said "In
your spare room." I ate some of the omelette. It tasted of
earth and herbs. The sea.

There is totality under drugs. You touch something and
it feels; reacts. Matter was alive. Charlie had his head back
against Anna's shoulder. I wanted to say—We know; what
more can be said. An arrangement of lights, colours: a
harmony with crystals. Time freewheels: Charlie was saying
"All upper class girls—" Anna punched at him. Charlie went
on "—all upper class girls are frigid." Anna's arms reached
for his hair, his face; to snatch his eyes out: strong brown
arms with weights at the bottom. Charlie dodged like an
old boxer. Gone slightly bald. "Ow!" Charlie yelled. The
omelette had gone cold: tasted of iron. Anna was a wardress
in uniform. Charlie was holding on to her hands. She was
cruel. He had lost his spectacles. She had kicked him on
to the floor. Grinning.

I went out of the kitchen and along the passage to the
hall. There were the chairs and the furniture and the provi-
sions left for the dead. Charlie and Anna had no suitcases.
There was a pile of letters by the telephone. No coats, be-
longings. I went up the stairs. In the spare room there was
the four-poster with the cover over it; underneath blankets,
sheets, pillows, mattress. Some powder on the dressing table.
No clothes. Under the bed, dust, moth in the carpet. The

curtains drawn. Through the window my car in the moon-light. Next door in the bathroom was a handbag with some dark blue paper inside it. A towel on the floor. The bath had drops of water on it. What else had I forgotten. The house which had seen, remembered.

Anna came through the door into the bathroom. I said "Are you all right Anna?" She said "Yes thank you." I put my hands on her shoulders and stared into her eyes. I could hear Charlie talking downstairs on the telephone. I said "What can I say?" A pink and white Rubens gone crooked with a huge flowered hat. Anna said "You are so kind." I said "We're all too fond of you." I made a face with my teeth bared. "We are of you" Anna said. Her eyes were quite empty. I wanted to lower my head on to her shoulder. Charlie was shouting into the telephone downstairs. He seemed to be ordering a taxi. I said "I'll never understand you." Anna said "Why not?" I said "Really?" Anna turned her head away. She looked hurt. I put a hand up and touched her cheek. Something had been done to my brain. I said "Dear Anna, I can't touch you."

I thought—I will try again. Over Anna's shoulder there was a medicine cupboard and a mirror. I said "I can help you." Anna kept her head away. I said "Are you all right, tell me." Charlie had finished telephoning. I could hear him coming up the stairs. I was leaning forwards, ruined. A shipwreck. Charlie came into the room through still water.

I went off again down the passage. I thought—This is infancy. A man sits on the edge of his bed and shakes. We are all going back to hell. For an experiment. The world goes on outside in coloured oil and polish. No windows.

This is a story about free will. We are all in fragments, disjointed. We have moments when it means something. I know nothing of Anna. We have a choice. The familiar things of my room, books, alarm clock, tumbler. Rosalind's coat. Her dressmaking dummy in the corner. I am half a person. A millionth. We think too much: stare at it. A body on a stand cut off at the neck with a wooden plaque. A long mirror hung from a central hinge. The problem of optics. The object and image. Your fingers crushed. I would go to bed. If you passed enough time, it was time to go to bed. The day was something to be filled in by doing things. Nothing else. Time became packed, like a suitcase.

In the early morning half way between sleep and waking there is a time like someone drowning; going down three times, coming up, then sinking out of sight to the bottom. Space settles round you like a formation of soldiers. This is all quite new. It has been there all the time.

The telephone was ringing downstairs. There was a taste of cold ashes in my mouth. My head ached. There was something not to remember.

Charlie had been on the telephone and had rung for a taxi.

I waited for Charlie.

The telephone went on ringing. I had been dreaming of Anna. In the cabin of a ship, an old sailing ship, the captain's cabin at the back. Like a cottage. I had sat on the edge of her bed. I had said "I will help you."

There was no one answering the telephone. Charlie had left.

I jumped out of bed.

Charlie and Anna had left in a taxi.

I took Rosalind's coat and ran down into the hall. The lights were on. As soon as I got there the ringing stopped.

I sat by the telephone. It was just getting light outside. In my dream there had been a long sequence round a table. Eating. My head throbbed. I thought I was going to be sick.

What had Charlie and Anna been doing.

I had sat by this table before.

There was the pile of unopened letters by the telephone. I had seen the letters as I had come through the hall.

What had I done so terrible.

One of the envelopes half way down the pile was in the writing of Charlie's wife, Laura.

I had forgotten Laura. I had thought nothing about her. I opened the letter.

Dear Stephen,

Forgive another point of the Eternal Triangle butting in. Of course I'm grateful if you're helping Charlie in this bloody situation, but what I'm horribly afraid of is the danger—at least I see it as a danger, but you may think this absurd—of your inadvertently making the romance or whatever the beastly thing is called seem even more real than it is. Whether in fact it's real, or what degree, is unanswerable—in a way everything is in the mind or imagined, isn't it? I suppose you know all about this. But I know Charlie's very susceptible as far as you're concerned. So what I'm getting at is, to beg you that while still being understanding, sympathetic, etc. you don't necessarily show to him you think it's the great thing of his life. You might even hint (terribly indirectly of course) that he would really sooner or later (probably sooner) be bored to death by her. I believe this madly of course, but naturally am in a wrong position even to hint. Does all this seem childish low cunning? But I do hope you see what I mean. It is terribly important.

I always wondered what this would be like if and when it happened. But I must say it beats everything for pain.
Love,
Laura.
P.S. Don't say I wrote for heaven's sake.

I had my mouth open. I listened. Laura was a pale brown-haired girl in a smock. She wrote with her head close to the paper. Upslanting spectacles. I wanted to cry. She had a lilting, appealing voice.

I thought—I am mad. Why are we made like this?

The telephone began ringing again. A voice said—"A personal call for Mr. Jervis."

I said "Speaking."

"You are Mr. Jervis?"

"Yes."

I was going through the other letters in the pile. There was one from Charlie. With a date on it. I couldn't remember the date. When had he come here? When had I gone to London?

I opened the letter.

A voice on the telephone said "Stephen, is that you darling?"

I didn't recognise the voice. I thought it must be Francesca. It was four or five in the morning.

I said "Yes?"

The letter from Charlie began—

Dear Stephen,
    Been trying to ring you. Could I come and stay. I'm so sorry for all this—

The voice said "There's nothing to worry about, but Rosalind's been just a little bit ill, and I thought I should telephone."

I recognised my mother-in-law's voice.

I said "Is she all right?"

"Dear Stephen, I think she's quite all right, but she's had a slight haemorrhage."

I said "But she's all right?"

"The doctor thinks she'll be all right."

"Shall I come over?"

"Darling Stephen, I think she would love it."

I said "I'll come right away." I felt a terrible ache. I said "What exactly does the doctor say?"

"He says she'll be quite all right."

"I'll be over in an hour or two."

"Darling Stephen."

"Tell her not to worry."

"Yes I will."

"Give her my love."

I put the receiver down. I looked at Charlie's letter.

I thought—It will only take me an hour to get to Rosalind. I have my case already packed, the car out, money. I can put my tutorials off by telephone. I will leave a note for the woman who comes in each day. I will be moving: everything is possible.

I thought again—I am mad. Shall I kill myself?
I moved through the house, to my clothes, bedroom.
Rosalind's white face. I went cold again. I sat on the edge of
the bed. I had slept with Francesca.
Rosalind.
I snarled. My legs wouldn't work.
I was a lunatic in the charnel house.
When saints met the devil they spat, farted at him.
I thought—Guilt is nothing. What do you do?
I went on dressing. My case, my coat. The only thing
man was good at: playing soldiers. In a crisis so calm,
rational. Destroying ourselves.

In the night air there would be that long road over the
hills away from London. Sitting in the car with the concrete
and the dark earth rolling. The stars out. Galaxies. Shooting
away from each other.

VI

18.

Rosalind was in bed with a high back of pleated yellow. Her face an unwatered flower. I said "My love, my angel." My head was still moving with the drive, the line like white arrows. The room was shaded. I said "The doctor says it will be all right." Her hand was soft, damp, a taste of metal in the evening. She said "You are good to come." I said "Of course I came." I sat down and felt her forehead. I said "Does it hurt?" She said "A little." She swallowed before she spoke. The steering wheel shook from the road; the bars and cogwheels. I said "My beloved." Her forehead was a cave with the rain in it. I said "Don't try to talk, just stay quiet."

I held her by the arm and shoulder. A power like electricity. Something going out along the hands and the leap of life. She lay as if there were no thickness in her. The child wrinkled. I could not imagine this. I needed some current: life in me.

I said "I'd been up in London; I'd just got back." I remembered I hadn't read Charlie's letter. The room had its curtains drawn. I said "I saw the television people, but it wasn't any good." I thought—I want to tell her; to start again. For my own sake.

We are such cowards.

She said "Did you see anyone?"

I said "No." For courage.

I said "I've been talking to your mother. You've just got to stay in bed. You'll like that."

A house with a garden of creepers and rhododendrons. Stone walls. A cottage.

I said "When did it start?"

She began clearing her throat. Painfully.

I said "No, don't talk." I put my head down. In the dark, that cold. Hanging on to her. The underground river.

I said "What else had been happening—"

I wondered if I could read Charlie's letter.

I said "Charlie's been staying. He turned up suddenly with Anna."

I sat up and took out the letter from my pocket. I began reading it. It was short with untidy writing.

Dear Stephen,

Been trying to ring you. Could I come and stay. I'm so sorry for all this, but I've almost made up my mind to leave Laura. You know who for. Could I come for a few days. I feel dreadful.

Love,

Charlie.

I said "How are the children?"

Rosalind said "What happened with Charlie?"

I said "Something extraordinary. He and Anna are having a sort of affair."

She was moving very carefully in the bed, pushing with

her hands below the bedclothes.

I said "Do you want me to tell you?"

She said "Yes."

I said "I got back from London and found them there. I didn't know what they were doing. Charlie had sent me this letter but I hadn't got it."

She said "What does he say?"

I helped her to make herself comfortable in the bed. Sheets and pillows.

"He says he wants to leave Laura, but he won't."

Rosalind looked angry.

I said "I stayed up one night in London and got back yesterday evening. Or rather this morning. And there they were. I was very tired. Rather drunk. I couldn't make sense of it."

Rosalind was trying to reach something. Pills. A vase of flowers. I had not brought her flowers.

I said "Let me."

Rosalind said "I do think Charlie's awful."

I said "Then I found this letter, and a letter from Laura. I've got to go and see Laura."

Rosalind had got herself propped on one elbow. She reached for a glass. I helped her with it.

Rosalind said "Why were you drunk?"

The back of the bed. The corner of the room with table, books lamp. In the car again.

I said "I'd just got back from London. I'd had dinner with Francesca. Do you remember Francesca?"

Sitting in front of a screen on which a road was projected. A blank.

I said "Charlie and Anna were extraordinary. They kept

abusing each other. Fighting. I suppose people do this."

Rosalind lay back in the bed. The road began to move past dangers, accidents.

I said "My love you don't mind about Francesca, do you?"

She said "Yes."

I said "I only had dinner. I've got to have dinner."

How brave.

I felt for her hand underneath the bedclothes.

I said "Charlie kept on tormenting Anna. She's got some hold over him."

Her hand lifeless. I began squeezing it.

I said "Then I tried to have a talk with Anna but it wasn't any good."

I thought again—I am mad. What has happened.

I said "My love, when is the doctor coming?"

After a time she said "I don't know."

"I want to see him."

She said "You did behave well didn't you?"

I said—"Of course."

She said "How terrible for Laura."

I said "It doesn't mean anything."

Rosalind's hand began to move in mine under the bedclothes.

I said "My love are you all right?"

She said "Yes."

I said "I did come straight away."

She said "Thank you."

I said "I can't imagine myself into other people's feelings."

She said "What'll you say to Laura?"

I said "Not to worry."

She began to cry. The tears from her eyes silently.

I said "My love."
She said "You haven't asked me."
I said "I have!"
I kissed her. I held her in my arms. Gathering it up. Huge.
I said "I asked your mother!"
She said "You do care?"
"Of course I do." I dragged at her.
She said "You don't think it could be hurt?"
I said "No."
She said "I think it is."
I said "I know it isn't."
I held her. Her eyes on the edge of the precipice. Horses.
The wind in fir trees.

We were going deep. I thought—I am no good at this.
This is what matters.

19.

You drive up to Charlie's house past lilac trees and a
courtyard where there is a litter of broken toys just like
our own. You ring the bell and a dog barks miles away and
no one answers. You go through into an airy house with
windows and small seascapes on the walls like Boudin.
There is the piano where Laura practises with her head close
to the music. Laura was not there. Once when Rosalind
and I had arrived for dinner there had been no one there
except the sound of a bath running upstairs, and when we had
gone upstairs there had been just the bath with no one in it
over-flowing on to the floor. I called—"Laura?" Houses have

a life of their own; the doors, furniture. I went through to the lawn where there were deck chairs and a tangled hose. Laura was in the distance in three strokes like an impressionist. The trees watery. I walked towards her. If you think too much about walking you fall on your face. Laura was in her apron and her upturned glasses. It would be easier to sing; to do a funny turn with the hosepipe. I started saying "I was just passing—" Laura and I have a habit of beginning to talk at the same time. She said "Where have you come from?" I said "That's what Charlie always says!" Laura has straight brown hair to her shoulders and a thin, intelligent face. She said "Charlie's away." She began to take off her apron. She wore jeans, a sweater. I said "I wondered." She was like an English girl about to feed horses: pony, sieves, a bran tub. She said "He's doing an article about prisons: at least he says he is." I said "Oh that's just as well." Laura suddenly shouted with laughter. I felt relieved. Women were wonderful. I said "I've just come from my mother-in-law's, Rosalind's nearly had a miscarriage." Laura said "Has she?" She had pale blue eyes; flat. I said "But she's all right." Laura said "I am sorry." I wondered if Laura hated me. There was this thing about women hating. A colder day with wind, birds, hopping. I said "I got your letter." Laura said "Oh did you?" I felt rather dizzy. I said "It'll be all right." Laura picked up a piece of hosepipe and screwed it round. She said furiously "What will be all right?" I said "It doesn't mean anything." Laura put her hand on her hip: her mouth in a red line. She said "Have you had lunch?" I said "Yes." I thought—I've been driving all night: I am too tired. I said "Oh Laura darling, why did you write to me then, didn't you want me to come and see you?" I heard my voice shaking. I made my face stiff like a tragic actor. She said "Yes." I said "Well what I mean is Charlie won't do anything unless you push him, this thing with Anna is a lot of balls." Laura said "How do you know?" I shouted "I know!" I was beginning to over-act, gritting my teeth and rolling my head about. Laura had been peering down the hosepipe. She said "Haven't they been staying with you?" I said "I was in London, they might have broken into the house for all I know." I thought—She might have meant the time before. I said "I only found your letter after they'd gone." I thought—I keep on saying this. Laura said "Well, have a cup of coffee or something." I said "As long as you don't push him it'll all fall flat." Laura said furiously "Why d'you keep saying I'll push him?" I said "People do." Laura had picked up the hosepipe again. She said "He says he's in love." I said "Oh everyone thinks they're in love!" It was an English summer day, cloudy and the wind in poplars. I would transfer the hatred on to myself. Did I think I was doing this? Laura said "You seem to see it as an intellectual problem." My face grew older: I should be hurt by this. I said "Perhaps it is." I couldn't think what was coming next. I held my head in my hands and crouched a little. I shouted "Oh God of course it's awful!" The hose-pipe was a thin green plastic going flat at the bends. I said "I must stop talking, I know I can't get it right." Laura was chewing her bottom lip. I said "How are the children?" Laura said "One's got whooping cough." I said "You play that one on him." I grinned. Laura said "What?" I said "That'll keep the old sod." Laura said "You do say extraordinary things." I said "You see, you've got all the cards in your hands."

Laura, thirty-five now, straight hair, blue jeans, good bones, clear eyes, a fair skin. Always truthful. That summer thick with green, with chlorophyll. You tot things up like a laundry list: make an effort, then the thing grows. I said "What else?" We began walking towards the house. Laura said "He says she helps him." I said "Ha ha." I watched my shoes. Laura went ahead of me into the kitchen. A good figure, thin, rather flat. I thought—Perhaps I should make a pass at her. Introduce confusion; change. I wanted to say—It's all so funny. Laura from the back. Something fluttering in sandals, with toes pointing out. Red nails rather dirty. She said "Coffee or tea?" I said "Coffee." I thought I should lie down on the kitchen table. Pretend to be dead. Laura said "Is Rosalind really all right?" I said "Yes." Laura said "I must go and see her." I leaned against the table. How long would I have to stay. Laura said "Thank you for coming." I said "Not at all." Laura said "You're not just being nice, are you?" I said "Yes I am." Laura did her sneeze of laughter. I thought I had done this rather well. I wondered where Charlie was. My head still ached. An empty area at the back on the left. Something to do with prudence. Cutting it out. Leucotomy.

20.

Charlie and Laura lived about an hour away from Oxford, somewhere south of Henley, which is about an hour away from Wiltshire where my mother-in-law lives. These three places formed a triangle in my mind;

123

on the sides of which I travelled steadily.

I found my house empty. The shoes and toys in the hall. I had work to do. Tutorials, a committee at five, rearrange what I had missed. Charlie would not have gone home: I would have passed him in the car. Analyse this. Eliminate. I was too tired.

The house had been cleaned. Breakfast was still on a tray in the kitchen. In the spare room the bed had been straightened. In the bathroom there was the piece of blue paper from a packet of cotton wool.

I had been over this before. Clues, or instinct, like a scent. Science.

I sat in the hall.

Charlie had not had a car. He had been ringing up for a taxi. He would have taken Anna where she could get in in the morning. In the dew, with her dress above her ankles. Wearing trousers. Taken her to the river. A Seurat by a railway bridge.

I thought—What does she see in him. A father; to be broken by.

A lecture to prepare. Committee.

I thought—Of course I'm jealous.

I went out to my car. My shoes and trousers on the gravel. I had noticed them before. Anna in a hayfield. A big blonde girl. I had put my hands on her shoulders. I had said—We're all too fond of you. Francesca had had her eyes shut.

I was on the dual carriageway going in to Oxford. How had I got there? I had been on the drive looking at my shoes. Charlie with his head on Anna's shoulder.

I must remember to ring up Rosalind. Would I ever feel

anything. Sometimes you drive for miles without being conscious of it.

Traffic. Shops. The cave of a restaurant high on a cliff. Where the dead were buried. Beads and feathers. Leaving the car on a pavement. By the walls of grey stone buildings.

I would say to the porter—Any messages? A man in a box with a board and desk. Would float along the cloisters. Remember something: stop. Open my mouth to shout and swear. Change it to a yawn. An eccentric. Becoming part of the scenery.

I said to the porter "Any messages?" He looked at his board, his desk.

Going along the walls a ghost, a skeleton, a cobweb blown up the face of a cliff. I could pretend to be this.

Charlie was asleep in an armchair in my room. I stood over him.

Charlie said "Oh Lord!" He gasped. He said "What time is it?"

"Lunch time."

He moved his jaw about. "Good."

"How long have you been here?"

He put his hands on the arms of the chair. Leaned forwards. Stayed.

I said "I had to go and see Rosalind."

He said "How is she?"

"All right."

I thought—I am quite brave.

Charlie said "Well, lunch." He stood up. Went to the window. He said "I've been here all morning, those bells, those bloody bells."

He was an old stork. Unshaven.

125

I said "Has anyone been in?"

He said "One sort of reddish person, medium height, a hockey player."

I said "You can move around your tutorials for a while, then people get fed up."

Charlie flopped again. He sat with his head towards the ceiling.

I said "Is Anna a Catholic?"

He said "Yes."

He shook silently with laughter. He shot up in his chair. He said "You're not her moral tutor are you?"

I said "No."

I thought—We are this new thing. A vacuum.

I said "Where are you staying now?"

"I don't know."

"You can come back to Palling."

He said "It wasn't me who wanted to go there. She seemed to know you were away. She knew Rosalind was away." He screwed his face up.

I said "William might have told her."

Charlie said "Oh."

I would have to get out of my committee. I would get a message to the porter. I would say Rosalind was ill.

I said "What's happening?"

Charlie said "I feel so frightful. So appalling."

I said "Don't."

Charlie said "No."

I said "It's just what you can do and what you can't."

I thought—This is absurd.

Charlie said "I could be happy with her."

I thought—The things people say!

I said "Of course I don't know what's been going on."
Charlie said "You can guess."
The thing coming out like a fish into the air. Dies.
I said "What does Laura want?"
"Well, to carry on."
"Does she know?"
"Most of it."
Charlie began swearing.
I said "Come and have lunch."
He said "I've never thought myself much of a—"
Charlie looked ill. His spectacles were broken and
patched with plaster. He had been married to Laura for
fifteen years. He had four children, thirteen to three. He
worked at home, travelled. Probably not enough to do.
I said "—of an expert?"
Charlie shrugged.
Laura came from a line of shipping millionaires. One
generation upper class. Consciousness. Bony.
Charlie said "I do really love her."
I said "Anna?"
Charlie said "Yes."
I began to imagine a conversation between myself and
Rosalind. Rosalind—But what did you say? Myself—
Nothing. Rosalind—Why not? Myself—You've just got to
let it take its course, not moralise. Rosalind—That can be
an excuse. Myself—But it works.
I wanted to say to Charlie—When did it start? You do
mean you have slept with her?
Charlie said "She wasn't a virgin."
I thought—Oh dear.
Charlie said in a bright way "What exactly is her rela-

tionship with you?"

I said "What indeed."

Charlie said "She's obviously fond of you."

An analyst sat slightly behind a patient out of sight. The patient talked. The patient both did and did not want to talk. A blockage.

I said "When did it start?"

Charlie said "After that party."

I said "What party?"

Charlie said "That Woodstock Road party."

I felt annoyed. I couldn't remember this. I didn't understand Anna.

Charlie said "I asked her to lunch."

"You pursued her?"

Charlie said "Flat out."

I laughed. I said "I didn't know." Two old men talking of girls can destroy anything.

I said "I envy you."

Charlie said "But she'd been sleeping with this man William first, so I haven't got too much of a conscience."

I thought—I know nothing. Thank goodness I have slept with Francesca.

Charlie said "She was extraordinary. We'd go to her room in the middle of the afternoon. Didn't even have a lock on the door."

I thought—This is disgusting.

Charlie said "What would have happened if we'd been caught?"

I said "I don't know."

Charlie said "We were once. Some ghastly girl came in."

I said "I expect she loved it." I thought—Flatter him.

"Then we had to find somewhere else."

"Me."

"Yes."

I thought—I make myself sick.

I said "What, that first Sunday she came with William?"

Charlie jumped up and held his head in his hands. He shouted "It's so awful, awful, awful!"

I thought—Stagger a bit more round the furniture.

"God!" Charlie shouted.

I thought—I've got to feel something. If you can't cry because you're sad, be sad because you cry.

I said "Don't leave Laura. You'd be crazy."

Charlie said "Of course it's the children."

I said "You break yourself. You know this."

Charlie said "Let's have lunch."

I said "I've got a committee."

"Oh, never mind then."

"No, I'll put it off."

"Are you sure?"

"Of course."

I moved around the room touching papers. I thought—I must stay with Charlie. Make a sacrifice for him. I said "A total moral collapse." I thought—Everything going quite well, really.

21.

There was a night somewhere around this time either at my mother-in-law's where I sometimes now stayed (thick

bed, pillows, suffocation of stuff) or in my room at home
forlorn as if there had been a death; when my sleeping pills
didn't work (those harbingers of spring) neither the first lot
nor the second, and the third lot wouldn't kill me, though I
didn't mind if they did, being a bag of old guts now, shot at
by the night, lights and luminous. Something rotting inside,
food, a great bog, cancer. Something swelling like a balloon
(once it had not been like this) making the soft things hard
and snap like drainpipes. Fall of dead leaves from an autumn
roof. I had lost the sense of body, the parliament of cells.
Something fallen into a ditch blind with myxomatosis. To
wish for destruction as a mercy; to be dissected on a slab.
The air was poisoned; the nettles woven into sheets. The
light an anodyne to destroy me.

Once it had not been like this. There had been the first
touch, the point of it. A body in the moonlight. The hard
white luminous thing. The blind man touching. The first
word of a child. Learning to grow in the cold air. Flames
on snow. Not melting.

Rosalind and I had been like this.

Now there was a bead curtain, a counter selling mealies.
I would roll over in my bed weeping. Girls with hair in
globes and cautious monkey faces. Sitting on trees and
searching through the bars for nuts. Quiet and virginal,
where love would be.

Rosalind and I were not like this.

Rosalind and I had met in Oxford when I was still
young—a story to tell to my children and my grandchildren.
Understand it.

I rolled on my bed, not sleeping.

Rosalind and I had met in Oxford when I was still young,

what it is to be young, walking in green fields, standing on
street corners, dust in your hair. Had felt so much then.
Like some irritation on the skin, pollen, causing violence.
I had stood on a hilltop and yelled: had crouched and prayed
for extinction. Oxford was a village unchanged since pre-
history; its ancients, ghosts, dead propped in chairs. At the
full moon people appeared in masks. Its priests, its power
and congregation.

Rosalind and I had met in the bar of an Oxford pub. She
was an apparition from beyond my mind, a myth, the white
flower of a cactus. A large girl with holes in her clothes. A
sort of refugee. I did not know these things: Charlie and
I had been moles, burrowing. Rosalind was a cathedral.
When one is young one does not see these as people. They
are things one comes across. A treasure or secret. To adore:
to give oneself to. Grey stone and crumbling creepers.

In the Oxford pub there had been woodwork, stains,
brass, glass. People talking with hands round their ears. The
leopard and the hunter. I looked down the sights. I thought
—The trick of memory. I have known her before.

In the Oxford pub. People playing darts.

I had said "Do you play darts?"

The whole animal kingdom brayed. Whooping of birds,
screams, gurgle of hippos. Monkeys crashing in trees. A
still lake.

When she moved she walked down an avenue, that stuff,
skirt, woven, cobwebs. A sort of mesh within which fish
lived and died. This scene, now, brass, glass, woodwork.
Rosalind and I had not seen each other before. I was trying
to pick her up in an Oxford pub. I was a scurrying thing in
a duffle coat: an arm on the bar, a counter. Moving to

and fro to music. I picked up darts. Wiped the slate. I turned to this tall blonde girl. I had the darts in my hand. Offered them.

She held the first dart with its feathers to the front and threw it with such force that it went over a high glass partition and disappeared travelling fast into the saloon. I thought it might have killed someone. I gazed after it: that diagram in space with thin and ghostly music. The man on a hilltop with machine guns. I said—You're holding it wrong. She said—How should I hold it? I showed her. The second dart followed the first, swinging over the wall beyond sight, beyond gravity. I only just remember this, the dream taking over, you have no power. Rosalind said— Is that right now? I said—It depends what you're doing. A man came in from the saloon with the two darts in his hand. A big red-faced man with red eyes. Rosalind thanked him. She threw the third dart and it hit the board in the double five. I went to the slate and chalked up the 301 and underneath it the 291. I went to the second of the two white lines on the strip of corrugated rubber. Put my toe there. The cigarette advertisement. Holding the dart in my hand. A small light wooden thing; weighted.

We do not feel this now. Love. To take off, flying. The tall blonde girl and the man in the duffle coat in the Oxford pub. The crowd on the steps of Odessa and the soldiers coming down in a line. Two refugees (Rosalind and my-self) inside the caisson of a bridge, listening. The girl not speaking much. The man older, a bit of an actor. I cannot visualise him. He always has his back to the viewer and his shoulders hunched. We have sharp nails with which to bury all this. The crowds outside the Tuileries. Grapeshot.

132

Rosalind was a soft flame in this hard world. Something so strong, beautiful. A pain in my heart at so much beauty. My hand shakes as I write this. There is so much sorrow, death. I adored Rosalind. The dream is more real. The perfect flower.

We are not like this now. What I remember are the physical surroundings of love: snow, heat, the edge of the sea. I remember myself as being involved in something separate; a child, a foundling with no parents. I lay in the lap of the earth and cried. I do not remember much else. And yet there was the whole landscape; a detail would show a different world. The towers, terraces. Now we watch the next generation of William and Anna. The old green thing. The touch of it.

Now we are older in our own rooms, our chairs. It has happened while our senses were not looking. All in our head. The connection between ourselves and them is only in stories. But in our dead villages with the old on our doorsteps what do we do, what do we wait for? To take off above the trees like witches; to be buried a week without air. A hand moves up and down in front of our face. A finger clicks. We are asked to wake up. We do not know if we can, there is too much suffering. Too much ecstasy. Do we ever have a choice. Our brain looks down on it. We want to kill what we don't have. So they won't have it.

22.

Anna said on the telephone—"Do you know who this is?"

I said "Yes."

"How are you?"

"How are you I should ask."

"Is your wife all right?"

I couldn't think what to say.

She said "Are you there?"

"Yes."

"I wondered if I could come and see you."

I was in my room, in college, with a pupil. I was working late that week to catch up with lost time. My pupil was a young man in red socks. I reached for my engagement book.

I said "Aren't you coming some time this week?"

She said "I wondered if I could possibly come before."

I had the impression there was someone with her the other end.

I couldn't find my engagement book. I pulled a blank sheet of paper towards me and pretended to write something. My pupil sat with his feet turned inwards. I started drawing diagonals on the blank sheet of paper. I said "I'm teaching till half past six, could you come then?"

She said "I'd love to."

When Anna came she was wearing a shapeless red dress with the waist somewhere round the hips. The skirt was above her knees. Her hair was fairer and smoother: it seemed dyed. Her arms and legs brown; her eyes paler, as in a negative.

I said "You're looking very smart."

She said "Thank you."

That soft rather pouting mouth. Eyes bright. I could never do anything except describe her.

She said "I never thanked you for having me to stay the other day."

I said "That's all right." I thought—This means nothing. I don't begin to understand her.

She said "I want your advice, rather."

I said "I'm not very good at it."

She said "Oh I'm sure you are."

I thought—Charlie's been talking to her.

She began acting with a cigarette. I thought—This might be the first time she has smoked. Girls have a sort of mindlessness about them. Coming out of their shells with petals.

She said "I'm thinking of getting married."

I said "Are you?"

"You don't seem interested."

"I am."

Puffing at her cigarette. "You said the other day that big things like getting married weren't important, what mattered were the small things."

"I said that?"

"Don't you remember?"

"No."

I was angry. I recognised something destructive.

The room, bookcase, red carpet, papers.

I said "Who are you marrying?"

She said "William."

I thought—Well that's all right.

Then—Perhaps real suffering might appear the same.

"Congratulations."

"Thank you."

Young. Inside her sack dress. Being carted off to the river.

"When did you decide?"

"The other day."

Waving smoke about on a stage.

I said "What about Charlie?"

She said "That was what I was going to ask you."

"What?"

"If you would tell him when you see him."

Myself alone with Anna. Distance about two yards.

She said "I'd just like to know how he is, what he thinks about it."

"You just want to know."

"Yes."

I made a gesture. My hands pointing up with the palms inwards. I said "Anna—"

She said "Yes?"

Hurt. Distrustful. Charlie and Anna had been staying at my house. Charlie had wanted to leave Laura. I had said he wouldn't. I had encouraged Charlie and Anna.

I said "This isn't a game."

"Of course not."

"What happened with you and Charlie?"

"Haven't you seen him?"

"No."

"I thought you had."

I thought—I'm lying. Then—She's a fool.

I said "I haven't seen him for some time."

Something fighting inside her. Cats.

I said "This is very difficult. We're going to get in a muddle here. What is it you want me to ask Charlie?"

"I'm very fond of him, and I'd like to know what he thought."

I said "This doesn't make sense."

She said "I think he likes William, don't you?"

Something utterly alone about her.

I said "You aren't seeing Charlie any more?"

"Oh I expect so."

"But you broke it off?"

"Broke what off?"

I thought—They slip into small bright spheres like mercury.

I said "Did you love Charlie?"

Anna puffed and blinked. She said "I wouldn't like Charlie to disapprove."

I said "Charlie—"

She said "I do care."

I said "Anna, we're to blame in this, Charlie is, but you're not at all. Charlie can look after himself."

She said "I expect he will if you tell him to."

I said "What?"

Some totally different girl. Angry. Throwing her head about.

I said "Anna. I know I've been to blame."

"He is your friend after all."

I said "Listen, what's happened is this. You've been hurt about Charlie. I'm terribly sorry. But you now want to hurt something back. I don't blame you. But not William. Don't make the whole thing worse."

She said "Oh you are moralising."

I said "Why marry?"

She said "I thought you were a friend of William's."

I said "Are you going to have a baby?"

She looked amazed. Then she said "Oh how English!"

I said "Then do you love William?"

She said "How sweet, do you think that's the only reason why people marry?"

I said "We're not getting anywhere."

I thought—Perhaps it would help her if I made a fool of myself.

I said "Of course I'll tell Charlie. But Charlie and I are much older, married, we've got what we want. You don't know about people like us. We can always go back when things are difficult."

I thought—Perhaps she really can destroy us.

She said "Why don't you want me to marry William?"

I said "I've told you."

She said "You couldn't be more wrong."

I said "All right."

She waited for a bit. Finished her cigarette.

I thought—I've done this wrong. I should have just listened.

She said "When will you be seeing Charlie?"

I said "I don't know."

I thought—I once thought she might be fond of me!

23.

I drove the forty miles again to where Charlie and Laura lived. The world of wives, secretaries, golf balls, officers. Heraldic signs like physics, sand and firing ranges, round-abouts and railway bridges. A demonstration like a toy shop. Trains went through mottled tunnels and ran past cows of brown and white plastic. Red racing cars moved with men in a permanently seated position. Behind counters were giant men invisible, leaning over roofs, solicitous.

I thought—Charlie is my past. We walk one behind the other in a sort of patrol.

Charlie's and Laura's house had its lilacs and paved courtyard. I walked through the hall with the broken toys and seascapes. Charlie and I strutting when we were young. Cocky: two-faced. I went through the house on to the lawn. Charlie and Laura were weeding. I thought—I have done this before. Not just the last time with Laura, but with Charlie. Charlie had his shirt off and a thin hairy body. He showed no sign of recognition. Laura was holding a wickerwork basket with wheels and a handle like a walking stick. There was the same hosepipe and the bright poplars. Laura looked up through her spectacles. I called for the hundredth time "I was just passing!" Laura's mouth in its thin red line. I wondered if she had told Charlie I had seen her. It did not matter. Charlie was holding the hosepipe out of which water was running slowly into a puddle. Laura wiped her hands. Charlie squeezed the end of the hosepipe so that water splashed into the puddle in jerks like a horse peeing. Laura shouted "Charlie!" Charlie stopped. I walked round the flower bed. They had a bed of magnolias with the flowers all gone. Roses. Pansies. Charlie screamed. Laura was holding a garden fork and seemed to have jabbed him with it. He was wearing a pair of blue serge trousers done up with string. His ribs showed through his skin. I thought —We are a trio of old professionals; a soft shoe shuffle in straw hats. Laura was squatting and weeding. Charlie tried to help her. Laura gave him a push and said "Keep your hands to yourself." Charlie fell back on his elbows. He said "That's my trouble, can't keep me hands to meself." He waved his hands about, banging the backs of them against his thighs. I said "Have some stuff put on them." Laura was on all fours over the flower bed. Charlie put a finger on her bottom and then screamed and thrashed his hands about. Laura shouted "Oh shut up Charlie!" I had tears in my eyes so that I could not see through my spectacles. I took them off and there was the changing scene, the bottom of the sea with green and silver weeds. Laura said "Have you come from Oxford?" I said "Yes." Laura said "Have you seen old pop-eye?" I knew what she meant. I was shocked. A chill from great depths. Charlie had his mouth open and seemed to have fallen on the grass from a height. Laura swivelled and stared straight into his face. She said "That old tart. German." The water was running out of the hosepipe and spreading towards Charlie's legs. Laura said "Why don't you wipe your spectacles?" She was talking to Charlie. I put my spectacles on and looked up at the sky. The light made a curve and a blue bowl. There was a buzzing in the garden, the leaves, paeonies. I said "I seem to spend my time driving between here and Oxford and my mother-in-law's." Laura said to Charlie "Go and turn the tap off." Charlie seemed paralysed. Laura began butting him on the chest with her head. I thought—This is some punishment: I am chained. Charlie rolled over on all fours and began crawling. He went like this right across the lawn. People rode like this on horses, old men in harness. Charlie turned the tap off. Their skin so thick they couldn't feel.

Laura said "Sorry, what?"

I thought—We are all too clever. We will soon be on our own, with our eyes shut. The brain in the frigidaire.

Laura said "Oh how is Rosalind?"

A child came out of the house and ran towards Charlie.

His little girl in a white frock and jet black hair. She climbed up on Charlie's back. Charlie began giving her a ride around the flower beds.

I thought—Now we are happy in the summer again.

I said "I seem to pass my time driving between here and Oxford and my mother-in-law's."

24.

Rosalind in bed among her flowers and pink pillows. The children hanging on to the bedclothes and occasionally pushing outwards on the floor with their feet like Sisyphus. Watching and waiting for some sign: from the goddess who dreamed them.

I said "My love, my darling."

Clarissa had kohl black eyes. I lifted her on to my knee. She put a finger up and touched my mouth, my chin. In a haze of sunlight. A lily. Courtesan.

I said "My girl, my baby beauty."

Alexander with his profile so kind and knowledgeable. He drifted round his memories of jealousy, incest. Beloved of the gods. On whose thin shoulders the world rests.

I said "And how have you been, Ali?"

I said—"I had to drop in on Charlie and Laura."

Clarissa rolled, pressed her head against my shoulder. Stroked her thigh. She pulled her knees up.

I said "I still can't make much sense."

Alexander leaned against me. He said "Daddy—"

"Yes my Ali?"

"When's mummy having the baby?"

"Soon."

"I felt it today. It kicked. It must have hurt terribly."

I held them and rocked them backwards and forwards.

I said "Charlie's not going to leave or anything like that."

Clarissa said "I see a river."

I said "What's in it?"

She said "Fishes."

I said "What else?"

She said "The fishes eat you!"

The room rich, upholstered. Rosalind in bed. A ditch and a palisade.

I said "How have you been my love?"

I had not been sleeping well. I had sinus from the summer.

I said "Anna says she's going to marry William."

I was facing away, holding the children on my knees.

When Rosalind and I had been in love, in that hot summer.

I had to have a change; to keep moving.

I said "I must go out for a bit. I've been rushing about all day."

In the garden, in the summer, this hot green thing, stifling. Thin silver hairs on stalks and white butterflies. At my mother-in-law's there was an orchard where if you lay down you disappeared. A forest of tall green knives. My head was like a singer transfixed on a pin. Above in the huge sky aeroplanes crawled. The ache in my head, chest, going out, flies and atoms. A dead mole with its feet in the air. The smell of metal. A knife swishing dust.

I lay on one arm in the position of the statue with holes in it. Through me the light looked into heart, guts. There was a cliff with strong sharp flowers and the sea roaring. Blowing spray about. My body on one arm soft as a landslide. At the bottom rubbish, old tins, the flywheel of an engine. Nettles through the rotting iron. Tougher than death, pale silver spikes. Old body that had worked as a piston.

In youth there had been the green time, in the grass letting insects crawl over me. Narcissus on his back with his reflection and the sting of bees. Around him white spittle in sick of energy. Now this waist, sack, seam. A lorry with its stuffing hanging out. Behind the dead driving wheel knobs, levers.

Around the world the starving, crippled, dung, milk, tears. The mother with her tadpole baby. The face wrinkled into wrapping for grease. The torture out of uniform, cat with fine teeth, rabbit hopping blind through twigs and brambles. The cat at the rabbit's neck finding pus, thin, a string of old bones, bladder. The cat looking up with one paw on its neck. A white tail. Girl in satin.

If you listened you heard suffering. The blood in veins and the rush of things growing. Flowers and the screech of trees. Like water draining off a glass, lips moving, head on a spike. The miraculous madonna.

This rushing upwards in a sort of song, a panic. I lay in the grass and had these dreams, spirits, bombers. These dusty roads and refugees. Looking up from the earth I saw this thing coming closer. The flowing gown and cap and silver hair floating up the steps of a crumbling building. I thought—I must go back now. Or else it would be too late. I would be inside that hall of flags and kings and mirrors, their arms parallel along the sides of chairs, waiting for electrocution. Smiling. Those beautiful creatures in museums. Outside the sort of rush, like the passover, splashing blood on doors. I tried to shake myself. From water. The smell of graveyards.

I went back into the house to Rosalind. I said—

"I'm so sorry, my love, I'm not very well. I've not been sleeping. This is a difficult time. Me being alone, you know, you pregnant; me going backwards and forwards always travelling. Also I've been working quite hard. Perhaps it's the summer, too, and this sort of age, I'm suddenly forty. We've been married ten years. Then there's all this thing with Charlie and Anna and Laura. I feel you disapprove. Perhaps you're right. But what can I do? What was I telling you? I went to see Charlie and Laura, you know, everything is all right. We had quite a good day. Charlie was doing one of his funny turns on the lawn with Laura pushing him. Acting it out, you know. Then I had seen Anna, just earlier, who said she was going to marry William. Well she was doing this to make Charlie jealous. She wanted me to tell Charlie, and I said I wouldn't. I was quite tough with her. I know I'm not to be trusted in this, but I think it was right. Earlier I'd had lunch with Charlie and he had been very good, really, but I've told you about this. I was underplaying it, listening. I think that was right. Then I had to work rather hard those few days. But it's no good taking a moral line, not because it isn't true, but because it only makes things worse. You know. I know I'm to blame. This is a very strange time. I think I've got to stop being a philosopher soon. I may leave Oxford. But what else?

"The person we've forgotten about in all this of course is William. I really must try to have a talk with him. I don't think Anna will marry him. But what can I say? I think he wanted me to be a sort of father-figure, but I can't do this any more, it's a deception. People have to be on their own nowadays. I don't know why, they just do. I can tell him things; but there's nothing to put into words any more. We don't know. Except in work of course, but this doesn't mean anything.

"This is what I think about, what I think is important. Either you turn into some sort of gutted thing, automaton, or you have to become involved with pain and birth again, the roots, and all that nonsense. I keep on saying this. But I do feel this sort of crack-up, everything exploding, we're one person one moment and another person the next; no continuity because no illusion. I'm a different person with you than I am with Charlie or in college. I don't know if this is good or bad—unless you've given in, unless you're an automaton. I don't mean this about you and me, we're all right, we're the same separate person. This is what marriage is, I think; it makes the rest of it possible.

"I know you're having the baby, darling, and you don't want to be listening to all this. But I feel such excitement sometimes! Such a change!

"Don't be angry my love. Yes you are, I can see it. This is the real thing, that I'll always be the same with you and the children. But I've got to have something outside to balance it—to discuss—this is part of the thing, that talking has suddenly become so difficult. Don't we all feel this?—Everything has to be gone into round and round; with its opposite.

"Do bear with me. I sometimes feel that out of all this something is being born—born everywhere—something to

145

do with us having the chance of being tougher now, not so haunted. We aren't so afraid. When we make a mistake we don't want to blame anyone, we don't feel guilty. We want to ask—What can we do about it?

"I know I talk a lot of nonsense. I still rationalise, try to justify myself. How much am I now? But it's a question of whether you trust, believe this; and then things go along with you; events, actions. Or whether you give in to a sort of death. I know this is asking for it! But what else is there my love? Do laugh! I do believe it!"

25.

On a cricket field like the Boer War, green and white, a promenade round a college cricket match. It was near the end of the term now, we were all tired, exams and parties. Young men and girls hung on like old boxers. Scattered about the grass like fallen statues. Tommy Parker and I were on the outside of the deckchairs, not looking at the couples in the long grass, watching them.

Tommy Parker said "Does the species 'bird' include the grasshopper warbler or cricket bird?"

Round the curve of a boundary a man in a boater, a bathchair, a sightscreen; then William and Anna in a group, approaching. Wearing masks; a street in Verona. In their black leather jackets and tights. One of my pupils with the red socks. All centred upon Anna with a white dress and parasol. Looking exhausted.

Tommy Parker said "*Die Marschallin mit ihrem Zug.*"

146

In a waltz where you turn and go back on the small stage I found myself opposite Anna. The bright music and thump of fifes. Bowing from the waist down with a hand at the back hiding something. A fish. William's face seen through water. Waiting to speak.

"I tried to find you."

"I'm so sorry I've been away. Did I put you off last week? When am I due to see you?"

Click of cricket bats. Cannon balls floating softly. Parents and grandparents. Red in the face and hairy.

William said "Can I come and see you?"

I said "Of course."

Anna pretty and lined like a *Comédie-Française* actress. About to burst into song and then stop like a faulty radio. Wrinkles round her mouth. Golden or make-up.

William said "When?"

I could not look at William.

I said "Yes do come and see me. When?"

His head coming out of the scrum. His ancestors and horses. Had I hurt him?

Tommy Parker said "When is the happy event?"

We all looked at the cricket match that was running down like clockwork.

William said "You're not supposed to know."

I said "Happy event refers to a baby."

The young men pretended not to notice. Cut off from us by a membrane.

I stretched my mouth backwards and forwards.

William said "Will you be in this evening?"

I said "I'm going home. What about later?"

Tommy Parker said "In Los Angeles, U.S.A., they call

it penial servitude, the insertion of the i referring of course to the more serious of the two conditions, unlike homo-ousian and homoiousian."

I was in profile, one foot forwards, a cowboy.

I thought—I must see William.

I said "Come out this evening."

He said "We're going to this party."

I looked at Anna. I said "The college party?"

Anna said "Aren't you coming?"

Anna in her white dress with the sort of gauze stuff round the skirt.

William with his arm round her waist. Claiming his package.

I hummed a tune.

The cricket was going on in a sort of mist on a distant plateau.

Anna said "How is your wife?"

I said "Much better thanks."

"Have you been doing a lot of driving to and fro?"

"I have."

William said "You do approve don't you?"

I said "Of course."

"No but really."

I looked at William.

"I'll be in till half past six. After that come out to Palling."

A detective.

Anna said "We'll have to change."

I said "You change."

William said "Your opinion means so much to her."

Tommy Parker said "Honest, Iago."

Tommy and I moved off again round the deckchairs. The

148

cricket was a sort of no man's land of green, a line of soldiers. I said to Tommy Parker "You know about Anna and William?" What had I said to William? William had said Do you approve? Tommy Parker said "An Oxford Abelard." I had said to William—I'll be in till half past six. I had meant I'd be in College till half past six. Tommy Parker said "And your friend Charles the honest broker." I didn't know anyone else knew about Charlie. I said "Heloise's father." I was being loyal to Charlie. Loyalty was what mattered. Tommy Parker had said—Honest, Iago. William had said—Your opinion means so much to her. The sun and the summer again. The trees like figures. The grass flailing.

Tommy Parker and I walked back through the hot streets. People on the corners wanting to fight. What happened when they couldn't.

Tommy Parker said "A statistical analysis of sexual intercourse among students at Colenso University, Milwaukee, showed that seventy per cent did it in the evening, twenty nine point nine per cent between two and four in the afternoon, and a point one per cent during a lecture on Aristotle's Analytics."

In the common room we were behind our magazines again. Like matadors. The sand and the dead eyes in the afternoon. The Provost hooded; a cobra of unshed skins. Tommy Parker with his feet up. There were sounds of the party being prepared in the courtyard outside: a tent, floorboards, the clink of bottles. The end-of-term party. Tommy Parker was reading the evening paper.

He said "Bookmaker found in undergraduate's bed."

The Provost said "Might it not be a misprint for bookmarker?"

We laughed.

I wondered what I could do if I left Oxford. Get away to the south, to blue and gold. Save up. Write. Put money in trust for the children.

The Provost took out his holder, looked down it, blew. He said "I remember once Provost Jones—"

He bared his teeth. He was a kind of grass, for a bayonet to be put into him.

"—when faced with some peculiarly recondite scandal—"

How much did Tommy Parker know? The skin of his face was woven, filled. We would go somewhere away from the bomb. That excuse for everything. The world in fifteen minutes. The sofa on which I sat of old cloth, sagging. A white thread in the green worn out by an architect. The Provost was saying. 'And black magic and the usual para-phernalia." We had put down our magazines. We were plugs, slots, on the face of a computer. The Provost had a little laugh somewhere miles inside; his eyes flicked like pointers of a seismograph.

A bell rang an hour. Traffic outside shook.

An appeal for ten million pounds.

I was wearing a pale brown jersey with two holes in it.

We were bicycling along a country road, up a lane of primroses. The chain had gone: our hands were greasy. Rosalind and I. There was grime on the flesh: you wiped your hands. Hot. A finger was torn off. The inside opening. White. Which was never seen.

The Provost said "So Provost Jones said '*Le coeur a ses raisins que la raison ne connaît point*'."

I said "What?"

Tommy Parker said "*Le coeur a ses raisins.*"

I thought—I ought to be seeing William. I had said—
I will be in till half past six. Guilt. Responsibility. There
was a tent in a courtyard. Summer with noises of corks
popping. Someone hammered with a mallet. William might
be waiting. I could get up: switch something in my brain,
walk. The thing that moved the switch was myself. Sitting
on a cliff with my legs over the edge. Currents flowing
from the brain, nerves, muscles. A gap between the mind
and the function. A man leaning on a high chair on wheels,
reaching for the face of the computer. The fall of the cliff
below him. Seagulls. Gorse growing out of the chalk face.

Tommy Parker said "Fourteen people killed in a football
match in Panama."

I said "Personal violence taking the place of communal
violence."

Tommy Parker said "Mayhem in cricket pavilion, Little
Puddleton eleven wiped out."

I could leave a message for William. It was so trivial.
All the old stories were trivial. We had been standing by
a sightscreen of slatted wood on rollers. There were boys
and girls in the grass. William's face had come out of the
scrum with his neck stretched. Perhaps I had wanted to
destroy him. Or he wanted to destroy me. Evil is compulsion. I was getting old. Too old for this sort of thing.
The seed in my head of a giant marrow. The summer buzzed
with ants, cathedrals. I was lifted out into cotton wool. A
free act. I need move my legs only if I wanted to. Or did not
want to. Sitting on the edge of the cliff. Waiting.

Rosalind and I could go to where there were trees with
long legs marching. A huge plain with tractors and corn-
coloured hair. Time was too big, too cosmic. Sandwiches

and wine behind a haystack. Anna in corn-coloured trousers striding with her shoulders back. The history of peoples moved across plains, across continents. Their cattle and oil wells. No future to it.

I had been sleeping. I was alone in the common room. I saw that it was after half past six. There was not long before supper.

VII

26.

Anna with one shoe off, her leg turned inwards. The cold around her (bitter on the tongue) in a room where murder might be committed. The four-poster, tasselled canopy, fireplace with tongs and shovel. We had to think very carefully. Anna was on her back like water-lilies; her skirt (green and white) above her knees. Lines of gold earth on dark stone. Charlie would be arriving within an hour. The road past the railway bridge, the firing range, the plastic cow. Man was a rat being experimented on for behaviour patterns. A passage, a bell, and a door which opened to warmth and food. Then the electric shock. The mind begins to shake. Anna's long legs inside her skirt like a bell. We throw away our chances.

William had been lying at the bottom of the car. He could have fallen from behind the steering wheel. Anna, falling on top of him, would not have made any mark. She would not have left anything. But if William had been driving it didn't matter if Anna was in the car. An unpleasant experience. Anna with her white bodice down at the front and triangle of white tapes, gold and wrinkles. I made a tutorial face with two furrows down my brow. William's face had been against the broken window at the bottom. The steering wheel was in the top half of the car. If his face had scraped against the ground there would be marks on the left side. He might have been thrown forwards and hit the windscreen or the driving mirror. Anna had trod on his face. The shock made you jump. Open to pure pain. I would give up. I would say—I just carried the girl, Anna—what should I call her?—to my house. I was tired. I would say this to the police.

I thought—We will all be ruined. Anna was drunk. Anna did not have a licence. The story of Charlie, William. I would lose my job. Anna would, or would not, go to prison.

I sat down by the edge of the bed. We had to think very carefully. If anyone had seen William and Anna leaving Oxford. If they had, Anna might have got out. William might have taken her home. If anyone had seen them on the road, the village. People make mistakes. If they had seen the crash. If Anna had told anyone she was going to see me. She could have got out.

My wife Rosalind. Alexander and Clarissa.

I was trying to help Anna. None of this really mattered. I was sitting on a chair a few yards from the bed. The skin under her arm was bunched, brown. A full skirt. What I had imagined. A last chance. Coming down into a cellar of padded walls, to do what you like there. A girl. All men are murderers.

I had encouraged my best friend to have an affair with my pupil. I had entertained undergraduates at night in my house. William was dead.

Anna should not be sleeping. She should be moving. Her brain was bruised. I should get a doctor. A doctor would say—I moved towards the telephone.

154

I had to think very carefully. The whole of a life, the lives of others. She had walked up the hill on her own. I had asked her—Are you all right? I had felt her skirt, her stockings. Her legs like the clappers of a bell. The shock of electricity and the trap door opening again. She was drunk. She was sleeping. After a shock you slept.

I was in a room with a four-poster and a fire. You see a different image in the mirror. You look and there is a room with ornate gothic windows. A man with an absolutely white face and a girl on the bed. Her face dissolving.

Charlie would arrive in half an hour. It would be the end of me. I would resign. I would go to the south to the world of sun and water. We had always wanted this. Or live on my own in a room with rats in the ceiling, my grey coat huddled on the desk. Rosalind and the children separate in a house in the country. William with his face empty and painted, lying on a table with the marks covered up. Where were the marks. If he had been driving he would have to have been leaning out of the window on the right side facing backwards. Anna on the underneath climbing over him. The man who had lifted William out of the car had not suspected. If they had, they would have asked.

Anna on the bed with her body coming out. The sole of a foot brown. On her front with one knee raised. A Boucher. The smell of girls. Teenage. Toffee sticking to the roof of your mouth.

Like Job, waiting. The world going past you. If you moved it would break. The roof of your mouth cracked. Five hours till morning. What should we do for love or justice. This was deeper than the mind. In blood; what we had all been feeling.

155

Anna would be taken to the police station. Perhaps she would not talk. Perhaps she had lost her memory.

There is a position in which you sit to make it easier to meditate. You sit straightbacked staring at a wall. A man comes behind you and hits you with a stick. Perhaps Anna would die. The shock of electricity again. They douse your head in cold water. They hold it there till you breathe, then pull it out. Careful, solicitous. You scream. They are trying to get at the truth.

27.

Charlie arrived making an enormous noise in his car that might waken the whole house and Anna. I ran downstairs and found myself holding the door open with a finger to my lips. Charlie said "What happened?" I said "William was coming to see me. They crashed." We went through into the drawing room. I switched on the electric fire. Charlie was wearing white tennis shoes. I said "He said he wanted to see me this afternoon, and I should have done in college but I didn't. Then he was coming here. I was asleep, half asleep, and I heard this noise and I went out into the lane and there they were. Other people must have heard it."

Charlie said "And William's dead."

"Yes."

"And Anna?"

"Anna's here."

Charlie looked amazed.

I said "I told you she was here!"

Charlie said "Why?"

I said "She was drunk. She didn't have a licence."

Charlie looked at me as if I was mad.

I said "I went down and found her on top of William. The car was on its side. The driving wheel was in the top half of the car. I helped her out and then I got at William."

Charlie said "But she was driving."

I said "She must have been."

Charlie said "Why in God's name!"

I said "She stayed down there when I came up to ring the police, then followed me. No, I think I asked her, I said— Come up to the house."

Charlie said "What?"

I said "She always said she wanted to drive."

Charlie said "But she's not hurt?"

"As far as I know."

Charlie said "But hasn't she seen a doctor?"

He looked furious.

He said "I'm sorry." He shook his head. "But they left her here?"

I said "They didn't find her. I found her."

I thought—Perhaps I shouldn't tell him.

I said "When they turned up she was here, up at the house."

He said "But when they saw her—"

I said "They didn't see her."

His face screwed up.

I said "Only I saw her."

Charlie began walking round the room. Quietly. The night quiet. He was listening.

Charlie said "So it's not just a question whether or not she was driving."

I said "No."

Charlie said "I'm terribly sorry about William. I didn't really know him."

I said "I was very fond of him..'

Charlie said "Yes."

I waited. I thought—It's he who's landed me in this.

Charlie said "But you said someone heard it."

"I didn't."

"Just now."

"Oh, I said they might have done. People came from the cottages when the police arrived. There was a breakdown-van and ambulance. But not before."

Charlie said "But they'll ask her."

I said "If they ask her at all."

Charlie said "They may never—"

I said "Exactly." My voice sounded like a lawyer. "In fact if they find out anything, they'll find out she was driving."

I said "What?"

Charlie sat down. He said "Begin again. They were both coming out to see you."

"From the St. Mark's ball. To talk to me, I suppose. About you and Anna."

"Did anyone know they were coming?"

"It's unlikely."

"Would anyone have seen them in the village?"

I said "This isn't the point. The point is when they ask us, or Anna."

Charlie said "I'm just trying to see it. Was there anything of hers in the car?"

"No. Or if there was, she might have left it earlier."

"Then when she came up here."

I said "No one saw her. I left her sitting in this room. Then when the policeman came she wasn't here, she'd gone upstairs. This is important."

Charlie said "What is?"

I said "I hadn't planned it."

I felt sick. I thought—I mustn't fall out with Charlie.

Charlie said "So you think it's a question of what Anna wants, or does."

I said "We can influence her."

Charlie said "Will she go to prison?"

I said "If they can prove the drink, yes, which they will. It was all over the car."

Charlie said "Then we can't do it."

I said "Do what?"

He said "You're against it, aren't you?"

I said "I don't know."

"Why?"

I said "First the morals. Second, it wouldn't work."

Charlie said "Why wouldn't it work?"

I said "We'd be accomplices. Perjury."

Charlie said "All right."

He looked exhausted. His eyes shut.

I said "Or perhaps no one would ask us any questions either."

Charlie said "Then what are the morals?"

I said "If no one asks a question we don't tell any lies."

Charlie said "Is that morals?"

I said "For God's sake, it's we who've landed her in this!"

He leaned forward. His teeth showing. I thought—He's trying to think I've landed him in this.

159

I began—"You don't have to tell the absolute truth every time without—" I stopped. I began again—"You have to trust that if you do the right—" I stopped again.

Charlie said "Well anyway—"

I said "I've been round and round all this."

We sat in silence. The dog appeared. Our black and white dog. Longing for company.

Charlie said "What'll happen to you?"

I said "I'll lose my job."

Charlie said "It'll probably come out about me and Anna.'

"Our little ones on the streets. Divorced. Starving."

Charlie began laughing.

I said "As a moral problem it's ludicrous!"

Charlie said "I suppose we just have to think of Anna."

I said "Or justice."

Charlie said "Justice."

I said "Abstract justice. The consequence for everyone."

Charlie said "Oh yes."

I said "I don't mean that Anna would in the long run be better off through expiation, though she might be. Nor us nor William."

"Then what do you mean?"

I said "One has to get back to the truth some time."

Charlie said "But not get out of the moral responsibility."

I said "And to run to the truth might be an evasion of responsibility."

Charlie said "Exactly." His voice copying mine.

I found suddenly that I hated this so much I wanted to give myself up. To be carried away and condemned.

I said "This is too difficult. Morals are too difficult."

Charlie said "What would you do if you were Anna?

160

Would you give yourself up?"

I said "I suppose so."

"But no one should make you."

"No."

"Then it's up to her."

"And our responsibility is to let her." I banged my fist against my forehead.

Charlie got up and began walking about again. He said "How long have we got?"

"Three or four hours. The police may come in the morning."

"But isn't it too late already? What have you told them?"

"I could say I was muddled, tired. I was."

"But about William."

"I said he was just coming to see me. And I could say I just wanted to talk to Anna first."

Charlie said "Why didn't you tell them?"

I said "I told you, that's just how it happened."

Every now and then there was a pure sort of fear, or guilt, a pain in the heart. I held my breath.

Charlie said "How certain are you she was driving?"

I said "Fairly."

He said "Did you ask her?"

I said "Yes. She didn't answer."

He said "She might not have been."

I felt myself sliding. I thought—What more can I say?

Charlie said "I suppose if she wasn't driving it wouldn't make all that difference."

I said "Of course it would."

Charlie said "To her, not to us. The rest of it would come out—you, me."

161

I thought about this. I said "You mean, if she wasn't driving, we would be protecting just ourselves?"

Charlie said again "Exactly."

I said "So let's hope she was driving, shall we?"

Charlie stared at me.

I said "Oh, it's funny. Think of William."

Charlie said "What's she doing now?"

I said "She's asleep."

Charlie said "Shall I wake her?"

"In a minute."

"We better not have a drink."

I said "Did you know Anna and William were engaged?"

Charlie said "That was all nonsense."

I said "She asked me to tell you."

Charlie said "I am very much to blame."

We sat in the drawing room. We seemed to be half asleep. Could not wake. Time was passing.

I said "This must be a thing that happens to people. We mustn't be beaten by it."

Charlie said "No."

I said "There must be a way though."

Charlie said "Yes."

I said "You better go and see her."

28.

In the hall, where the toys were, a grandfather clock, coffin, pendulum. The inanimate world that could outwit, outlast us. I wanted to mourn William. Wanted to say—I never knew you very well, never loved you. If this were possible.

Wood, iron, bricks, stone, plaster. Man was a maker of machines, communications. What he was good at. Could never touch a person. Only build a memorial. I had talked to William in my room with the bright lawn. The corridor in his house with the plumes and wild horses. I should have loved him earlier. Dying in vain. A platitude.

We can none of us feel anything any more.

There had been a tune running through my head for days now, something from Beethoven, falling down in phrases like water, infinitely tragic. From the third symphony I think; stately, a soldier. I wanted to say—We know it all now: the tramp of armies down the dusty road, boys with their hands in the dust, girls with one foot raised to sell themselves. Could I squeeze one tear to my eye. Or act a part, gesticulating. William was dead. I had tried to love William. I would throw myself into the grave after him. Play with a skull. The camera from above, swinging on a moonbeam.

What could I do for William. In the hall, empty room, empty house, night. Waiting to hear some pin drop from the universe. William lying on a slab with his spirit gone. All his ancestors and ancestors with a fury in the brain, their fingers. His face coming out of the scrum. A hair's breadth one way or the other. Planets fall, crash, the end of galaxies. If I tried hard enough I should be able to love William. Myself was nothing; a pendulum; a future hung from my side. My mouth a fish. Pyramid.

Something had to happen now. I could not live with what I had done to William. This is when we give up. Guilt.

The fakir under the earth for ten days. His problem—how to die quicker. The thing with its teeth on the outside; nails, hair, still growing. The row of bodies in the common room. Something had happened to them, once, something had died. Like me. The ghosts moving past the walls of old and crumbling buildings. I would become one of them. William.

I was standing in the hall, the dead time, four o'clock in the morning. Nothing at the centre, not even pain. If only I could cease. Listen to the clock. A wind. The wind stops. I hear a noise like a breath expelled through a dry throat. Then nothing. I wait for it to be repeated. Nothing. Nothing about death. Nothing to be done about death. Stay still. The earth comes down. You are buried. If you are still alive, the terror. Someone has made a mistake. You can't die. I listened.

29.

Charlie came down with Anna holding her with one arm around her shoulders. She had her mouth open and seemed to be caught in a tragic photograph. Charlie made a face with the lines on his neck stretching out. He sat Anna in a chair. She turned at an angle and looked at a corner of the ceiling. Charlie said "How do you feel old girl?" Anna took a breath. Charlie held her hands on her lap. He knelt down in front of her. I said "Would she like a cup of tea?"

Charlie was still kneeling and holding her hands. He had lowered his forehead against her breast. I poured out the tea. Charlie said "My cherub." Anna was breathing rather faster, swaying backwards and forwards. I said "Was she asleep?" Charlie took the cup. He said "Cherub listen." She seemed to be hearing something at alternate corners of the ceiling. He said "Just say yes or no when I ask you."

Like the frightened horse. The smell of precipices.

Charlie said "Did anyone know you were with William?"

She became still. A mirror to the lips.

Charlie said "Did anyone know you were with William?"

She looked straight at the back of my head. A man there riding with a red flag.

Charlie said "She doesn't hear."

I said "Of course she hears."

Her head went back. She seemed to start swimming, pawing. Her eyes closed.

Charlie said "We can't do this."

I knelt down. I said "Anna—" I was too close to Charlie. Almost pushing him. I said "William's dead. You had a crash. Were you driving?"

Stillness. The room ticking. Furniture.

I said "No one knows yet. You've got to help us."

She opened her eyes.

I said "Were you driving?"

Her head fell forwards. Charlie caught her. An impression of water rising past the eyes, the mind.

Charlie said "She's fainted." He held her head against her knees.

I said "She's not fainted."

Charlie's hand was on the back of her neck, pressing it.

I said "Anna—"

She made a choking sound.

Charlie put his head in front of mine. A blown up photograph. Huge pores. He said "She's going to be sick."

I said "Then get a bowl."

I put my hands up to my temples. Pressed them.

Charlie turned back to Anna. The tea upset. A stain on the carpet.

I said "All right Charlie."

Charlie said "She's got her life!"

I said "It's not me who'll wreck it!"

Charlie seemed to spin away in a rage.

I put my hand on the back of Anna's head. To do something.

I felt her breathing. Like a ship at sea with a storm coming. Huge drops. Her head began to toss from side to side. I pulled it and held it with my hands on her cheeks. I thought—I know what to do. She jerked her head back so that it hit the back of the chair. My hands followed it. I thought—There are lots of other things I should have asked her. Her head was going from side to side as if someone was hitting her. I said "All right Anna." She was making a chewing noise. Her body soft. Trying to find something for her head to hit against. I said "It's over now." I put my thumbs on her cheeks and squeezed them pulling her face out of shape. The eyes went into white slits upwards. I said "We'll do it all for you". I pressed her face against the side of the chair. Her hands were clawing in her lap. I pushed my body between her knees, my elbows against her arms. I tried to look into her eyes. I thought—Love. Power. After a time I relaxed my grip a little. Her hands had stopped clawing. I said "Charlie will take you back." Her body had become limp. I looked towards the clock. It was five o'clock.

I said "Have you got any sleeping pills?" Charlie was mopping up the spilt tea with his handkerchief. Charlie said "No." I said "I'll get some." Anna was sitting with her eyes closed. I said "Have a good sleep." I watched Charlie. He was picking up tea leaves and dropping them into the cup. I said "She can get in, leave her till lunch time." Charlie said "But the police." I said "I'll go and see Rosalind, I'll say she's ill. That'll give us till lunch time." I let go of Anna. I said "Have you got her bag and scarf?" Charlie said "Yes." I put my hands to my head and held it. I said "What else?" Charlie said "The sleeping pills." I said "Oh yes." I stayed squatting on my haunches. It was getting light outside. There was the wall and the flower-beds and the gravel. Charlie said "Do you think this is right?" I said "I think so." Anna did not seem to hear anything. Charlie leaned over her. He said "Come along old girl." He started lifting her. Nothing seemed to be happening. I thought—I can say I was so anxious about Rosalind.

When I came back with the sleeping pills Charlie and Anna were at the door. I gave them to Charlie. He read the instructions. Anna was standing beside him.

After they had gone I thought—I have not arranged where to meet Charlie. I sat down. What else had I forgotten?

30.

In the early morning I stopped in a lane, a wood, just off the road to my mother-in-law's house. In my overcoat and grey trousers and thick black shoes. There was a track up through scrub and nettles. I thought—I will have to telephone William's father. In an hour or two, after seeing Rosalind. The track went up past a wooden hut, padlocked, with its hinges off. The police would have told William's father. And the Provost. The thin noise of a tractor. An English country lane with mud, ruts, cow-parsley, beech trees. The world breaking up. Hazel and hawthorn. The names of birds and flowers. I would go to the Provost before lunch. I would say—Rosalind was ill. I would tell Rosalind. What else would I tell her?

I sat on a log. The clear morning air so still, so beautiful. I should make some bargain with God. Sitting on an anthill. That tragic man, Greek. A ragged daughter.

There would be an inquest. We had already done too much. We had tried to protect Anna. We had made ourselves responsible for her. Might make it worse. If anything could be.

A globe with a solitary man sitting on it. Screwing his face into focus. Pain. A five minutes' rest in war. Seeing the flowers: insects.

I thought—I have done all this before. About a week ago, I was doing exactly this. Driving to see Rosalind.

What is the difference?

William.

Something cracks in your life. You are finished. The world cracks.

But we could not have rung up the police and said—Here is Anna: we will bring her round to you.

I had been someone safe, hiding behind my walls and roses. The house with its bars across the windows. In the wood there was the hut with a pot hanging from three

168

crossed sticks. A princess running through the oak trees. Inside the smell of cloth, of excrement. Like dry fruit bursting. The rattle of shed snakes' skins.

The police would come knocking. William would be lying in some room in hospital. Anna would have climbed in and be undressed. Charlie would be driving out into the country, into some wood in the morning. William's parents would come into Oxford to see him. A room with bare white tiles. Charlie would ring up Laura. He would say— what would he? Laura with her trolley of weeds and flowers.

When you cracked, something decisive happened. We knew this. You either stayed defeated or you grew through suffering. How impossible it was. What happened to make you grow? God as a computer. The tossed penny in the air. Coming down on the connections. Fusing them.

I sat on a log in the early morning. Petrified. The air was pure. A few birds singing.

31.

My mother-in-law had a cook who lived, appeared, in a small window, framed, by the back door where you drove up, got out of your car, on gravel, slammed the door, crunched, began moving up the small paved path in the early morning. The cook's head and shoulders were framed, drying something or peeling. I smiled at her to explain my early arrival: I thought that I should try to seem cheerful. I went up the path of wistaria, or clematis, or something. Stone and concrete. The cook watched me. The door had a round iron knocker on it. The cook said "Mr. Jervis!" I said "A bit early!"

I was unshaven. She was a big grey woman with shining eyes. She said "So they found you!" I said "Who found me?" She said "They tried—oh—ever so many times!" I wondered if I would go back to the path in the wood; the police cars on the road like counters. I thought—How did they find me? I said—"Who tried?" The cook said "It must have been about six or seven." I said "But I was out. I started early." I thought—But I am saying that this was because Rosalind was ill. But the cook would know that Rosalind wasn't ill. The cook seemed to be looking beyond me: invisible lips, hairy. I said "How had they heard?" I pushed against the front door. I was frightened. The cook called "But they're not here Mr. Jervis!" Turning round I said "Where are they then?" Annoyed, efficient. I had nothing else to lose. The cook said "At the hospital." I said "What are they doing at the hospital?" I thought—William is dead. Then I thought—Rosalind. The cook said "Do you want to see the children?" I said "What's happened?" There were the birds. The air clear as a spanner. The cook said "They took her in an ambulance." I said "I didn't know." I began walking back down the path again. Something awful had happened. All this had happened before. But William. The cook said "Can I do anything Mr. Jervis?" I said "Have they taken her to Oxford?" Through the window there was draining board, sink, mop, detergent. The cook said "I think so." I said "I should have passed her on the road." I began tapping my foot and making a face like groaning. I had been in the wood. I had been going to say that she was ill. I said "Thank you Mrs.—" I couldn't remember the cook's name. I went on towards the car. The road going back like a switchboard over the downs. I stopped and called back "But how was she?" The cook said "Not too bad," I said "Thank you." The cook said "Shall I pack up some of her things?" I didn't know whether or not to pack up some of her things. The paving of the path was of stones and cement. I said "But it had just started?" The cook said "Yes." I thought—Why was I going to say that she was ill! I was about to step into the car. I was about to smash something. I would pull up the stones with my fingers. I said "Thank you Mrs.—" I couldn't remember her name. I sat behind the driving wheel. I could not drive. I could not get the car into gear. I would drive it into the wall. Fast. Now this was the moment. Quietly.

32.

A small brown room with two modern armchairs in it, a table, a high window. A sort of bathyscope at dawn. Four paces from the wall to the table. Four paces back again. A picture of a mountain-side with a fir tree. Putting your head out into the waste. A hospital. Pipes everywhere. The patients out of sight. Eyes looking out of a ground hole. Nothing living. No imagination.

I thought—Now I understand why people want it. A mechanism like a clock. Bomb.

A waiting room in a hospital like a strait jacket. Four paces each way. Yellow dust. Centuries of men and women. Children out of sight, crying.

Footsteps in the corridor. I did not want to hear them.

I thought—The executioner.

The door opened and Charlie came in.

Charlie said "Well well well well well!"

I said "This is loyal!"

Charlie said "How is Rosalind?"

I said "She's all right. The baby may not be."

Charlie said "I am sorry. But she is! How wonderful!"

I said "How did you get here?"

Charlie was prowling about ash-faced. He said "I got on to your mother-in-law's cook."

I said "So did I!"

He made a sneezing sound. Laughed. He said "I thought you'd been arrested!"

I said "So did I." He sat down.

I said "Rosalind was brought here at six o'clock."

Charlie said "But she's all right?"

"Yes."

Charlie said "I am so sorry."

He looked very tired. He seemed to have bars of iron in front of him.

I said "How are you? How is everything?"

Charlie said "Oh well, she got in all right."

"Nothing else?"

"No."

"What does she say?"

Charlie said "She seems to be leaving it to us."

I thought I heard something in the passage again. A trolley.

Charlie said "What's happened here?"

I said "The baby's born."

Charlie said "Born."

"It's in a sort of tent. I haven't seen it."

"How early was it?"

"Five or six weeks."

"It should be all right."

"I don't know." I blinked.

I said "Nothing about the police?"

Charlie said "No."

"Perhaps I should ring them and say where I am."

Charlie said "I'll do it."

I said "Thank you so much."

We sat in the two chairs. Arms along the sides. There was no air.

I said "It's a boy. One of its lungs won't open."

Charlie said "But they're certain Rosalind is all right."

I said "I think so. Do you think you could get a message through to the college too?"

Charlie said "Certainly."

Someone was coming towards the door again.

I said "This is fantastic."

Charlie said "Yes."

I said "I've been here hours. Nothing happens."

Charlie said "Have you had anything to eat?"

I said "I had some coffee."

Charlie said "I'll go out and get something."

I said "No. Thank you for coming."

Charlie said "That's all right."

"What did Anna say, did she say anything?"

Charlie said "She was terribly bruised."

I said "Poor Anna."

Charlie said "The baby'll be all right. They can do things."

173

I said "I hope so. I don't think it will be."

There were footsteps again. I tried not to pay any attention. A nurse put her head round the door. She said "Mr. Jervis, will you come along now."

33.

Rosalind, a sound of ticking, feel of rubber, on floors, wheels. Dripping white things. I said "My beloved, my angel." Walls went in and out. Hot. Leaning over her. Her doing nothing.

I thought for the hundredth time—This has happened before.

She raised a hand an inch. Listening.

She whispered "What were you—" In terror. Agony.

What was—?

She cleared her throat. Took hours.

I said "I was coming to see you!" My love! My darling!

"You couldn't—"

"I was! I arrived when you just left!"

"We rang you—"

I had been all night at a party. I had driven off with a girl in a car. I had crashed.

I said "Darling! I was coming to see you! I started off very early to your mother's. I waited a bit on the road, because I didn't think you'd be up. The thing is, something awful has happened. William's been killed in a car crash."

Her face became stronger. She looked at me. "William—"

"He was coming to see me. He crashed at the bottom of the lane. I found him there."

Rosalind said "How awful!"

Her hand began pressing mine violently.

I said "Now don't worry about this. We're all well, the children are well, you're going to be fine, my angel."

Tears came into her eyes. Rolled down her cheeks.

I said "I didn't know whether to tell you, but I thought I would as you're looking so well."

She said "I am so sorry."

I thought—I'm going to break.

I pulled up a chair. I said "Is the doctor nice?"

She swallowed. Cleared her throat again.

I said "I'll see him."

She said "Have you seen—"

I said "No. Don't worry. It'll be all right."

She said "It can't do anything."

I seemed to be looking down a valley of stones.

I said "This is one of the best places."

She said "They picked it up so roughly. They must have hurt it."

I said "They don't hurt it."

She said "It's so tiny. It doesn't have enough skin."

I began to rock backwards and forwards. Hitting the ground. My eyes open.

I said "Don't think about it now."

She said "Will you see it?"

I said "Yes." I started to get up.

Her hand held me.

William at the bottom of the car. Blood on the ground.

I said "I've been a bit worried about William."

175

Her hand still squeezing mine. Life. Energy.

I said "We'll go away for a holiday. We'll go to the sun."

The blood was on his left side. He couldn't have been driving.

I chewed at the air.

I said "Have you got everything?"

She said "I feel so terrible."

I said "We've got each other." I thought at last I was going to cry. I held her hand against my cheek. It was very cold. I said "You'll soon be better."

I put my head against her shoulder.

I thought—Never.

Dark room. Sheet over her mouth.

I said "My beloved."

She said "You do love me."

I said "Yes."

I stroked her cheek. Blindly. Something so soft.

I said "Does it hurt?"

She nodded.

I said "Where?"

Trying to move with her hands. Could not.

I said "I'll get someone."

"No."

"Now, you're going to get better."

"Tell me."

"What?"

"How it is."

I started to get up. I thought—I am broken now.

She said "They won't tell me."

I tried to get to the door. It was very difficult. I said "I'll tell you."

176

34.

A tiny thing in its tent, tubes, a shrimp, beauty as angels. Lying on white stuff making it raw. To be loved and adored. Sometimes a shudder or heart beat seemed to go on around it; inside the air, the bubble, that breathed. Something wrinkled and hard at the centre that wanted to die. I said—Let it not. Breathing with its lungs outside it, a sort of sky. Like the brain I had once seen in the Oxford frigidaire; not daring to ask who is it, what is it. Fearing to live. I stood and looked at it. Something new, a head, hands folded. Outside the forest with monkeys and cries of birds. On a bed of grass with its skin not properly finished. I thought—What shall I do. For so much beauty.

A plastic floor with curtain rings and rubber wheels and a cylinder. I thought—I can do something with my mind. I can move that small head, its circle, its dream to make it grow. The air comes in now and the body blooms, the seeds in millions. There is the bird-song and sun. You know this—no word—the world opens. Legs like a tiny fish, the long strong back. A line from me to it. Head. Showering water upon it. It moved its mouth, tasting. Its eyes fast shut. I thought—I am altering; altering it.

Some nurses moved. It was as if I were rooted within the earth with my eyes just flickering to show I was alive. I sighed. It sighed. You hear things. The spirits live in stuff imprisoned. You hear them sing! Their whole world flies up. A great peace. Having been liberated.

I began thanking the nurses for letting me see it.

35.

Anna's room which I entered for the first time had a lot of picture-postcards on the mantelpiece. There was powder on the chest of drawers, a guitar, the bed unmade, a pile of letters, an open suitcase.

No one there.

A girl's room. Some packing half done. I started to touch things: leaving fingerprints.

It was now the middle of the morning.

The old letters were on blue paper, underside up. I lifted them to see the writing. Thin and spidery. Not Charlie's.

I sat in an armchair.

There were footsteps on bare wood, distant, legs, a women's college. Blue skirts and tennis rackets, ankle socks and flour. Past the delphiniums.

Charlie was in the room.

I said "I keep on falling asleep."

Charlie said "She's getting a tremendous amount of sympathy."

I said "Why?"

Charlie said "Well, they were supposed to be engaged."

I said "Yes I see."

Charlie said "Everyone rallying round. They're sending her home by air."

Charlie seemed very bright. Excited.

He said "Tickets. Taxis."

There seemed to be a fly crawling up and down his face.

He said "I'm here for God's sake to help her pack!"

I said "As an old friend of the family."

Charlie said "An old friend of the family."

It was hot. The sun came through square panes of glass. It fell on the carpet in rhomboids. Narrowing the angle to a point.

On a beach with wild palm trees. Cocoanuts. Anna in khaki trousers. A wooden boat. Silver sand. White cotton.

Charlie said "Wake up!"

I said "Give me a few minutes."

I would have to ring up William's father. Would have to see the Provost. I would resign. Would drive down and sleep by the river. Willows. A punt with a white dress in it. Houseboats. Their shutters closed.

Charlie and Anna were whispering. They had their backs to me. I thought if I stayed still I should hear what they were saying. They were putting things from a drawer into the suitcase.

Charlie said "How are you feeling?"

I stretched.

Charlie said "You must be jolly tired."

I said "Hullo Anna."

Anna said "Hullo."

I said "Did you have a bit of sleep?"

"Yes thank you."

She was carrying piles of clothes. Stately. A sort of coronation.

I began waving my fingers to attract Charlie's attention.

Charlie came and leaned on the arm of my chair and put his cheek close to mine. A threadbare carpet.

I shook my head.

Charlie went back and stood beside Anna.

I felt in my pocket for a piece of paper, found my diary, tore a page out, and wrote on it *There'll be an inquest.* I waited for Charlie.

Charlie took the bit of paper.

I said "You're going home, Anna?"

Anna said "Yes." Stopped in the middle of the room carrying underclothes, a nightdress.

Charlie made his face with all the muscles of his neck standing out.

I pretended to go back to sleep again.

I thought—We've made ourselves irresponsible now. The heat like balm, golden.

Charlie said "Why don't you go back to Palling?"

I said "I will."

Life coursing along underground. A river through caverns and gorges.

I opened my eyes and saw Anna standing above me. Charlie was not there. I said "I keep on falling asleep."

Anna said "I'm going now."

I sat up. I moved my jaw round and round.

Anna said "I do hope your baby's all right."

I said "Thank you. How are you, Anna?"

She said "I'm all right."

I said "Good." I looked. That hard expression. I had been fond of her.

I said "We'll get over it."

I yawned. I made a little noise like a donkey. I said "Will you be coming back next term?"

She said "I don't think so."

I said "That's a pity."

She seemed to be waiting for something else. Her hair scraped back. A tight blue suit.

She said "Thank you for being so kind to me."

I murmured.

Big blue eyes. Searching.

I said "That's all right Anna."

She said "Goodbye then."

I said "Goodbye Anna." I stood up. I put my hands on her shoulders. Full red lips. Rather flattened nose.

Put my arms round her. A clumsy gesture.

I said "I'm off." I let her go. She stood in the middle of the room. A big girl. Rather beautiful.

36.

Now was the hardest time: man with his pretences, rationalisations gone: what is there to do, how is life possible.

I went to William's house with the portraits in armour and wigs from Blenheim, the thin moustaches from Mons William's father a quiet man gliding about in braided slippers. He took me by the arm so I knew everything was all right. Into his study, booklined, an insulation against heat: a grey man with a small head and face of a lizard. He said "I understand from the police—" Bronze statuettes, clock, leather blotter. Having lived through this ten thousand times before; at Agincourt, Hastings, Priam on the walls of Troy. He said "I know how much he valued your friendship."

Those gentle eyes not seeing anything, blinded by gas, softened by smoke and wire. Chairman of the bench, president of the waterways committee. I said "I only wish I had helped him." An aristocrat. How much did he want to hear? He lived in a silent world like fishes. Cut flowers, decanters, photographs of royalty. We can help by deceiving: help ourselves by helping others. I had an ear to the ground. No trouble; no publicity.

I never saw William's mother. She might have been in bed, a pink thing drugged, a royal bridesmaid. Or with her lover, some smooth torpedo. William had not talked about her much: had said he hated her. I could say to them—You killed him. Which would have been untrue. With their wigs and armour, in their house like caged reptiles. The sand and hot pools and the bright green smell. I was given a glass of sherry in a thick glass. I wanted to say—I loved him too. Which would have been untrue. I had been so tired all this summer, what with my wife having a baby. Our last before winter again. I looked out on to lawns and terraces and oak trees. William's father said "His elder brother, you know, was killed in the war. His mother took that hard." An understatement. I had to stay for twenty minutes. There was the sun outside and sound of mowing. The difficulties of youth today: the restlessness of the modern world. William's father said "I hope you will not blame yourself." I said—Nothing. We look through a slit in a turret towards fields and buildings and poplars. I was grateful to William's father. I had nearly achieved it: that shadow against the wall. I was given a handshake. I moved along corridors and out on to gravel. William's house lay in its park like a wounded animal; a carcase in the long green grass of the plain.

The Provost received me in his room, his green room lined with books; put his hand on my arm so I knew it was all right. This scene would be repeated for ever. We stood by the fireplace with the small marble statues with curved legs and decanters. He said "You'll go to the inquest?" His kindly domed head and his hooded eyes. He was always walking away from me, turning, suddenly re-approaching. He said "Of course I understand your feelings." Had been in the college for four hundred years; his name scratched on walls, grass, lavatories. I sat down. He gave me a glass of sherry. I was always sitting, watching, waiting for the enemy in their trenches. The Provost said "He was your friend as well as pupil." But I was one of them now, not the enemy. Perhaps they had all done something. The guilty. In clubs; power. The Provost said "But I think it important not to overplay it." The Provost and his daughter Francesca in the bath in Trinidad. Myself and Francesca in a room off Baker Street. We were in the net. Calm and quiet. Blue suits and stuff like cobwebs. The Provost said "That he was coming to see you was not unnatural." Out of the window there was the thousand-year-old graveyard: Provost Jones with his tall hat among the tombstones. I said "I think I should resign." The Provost said "I can see no reason whatever." I knew all this. Inside these panelled walls, corridors, the portraits with crimson down their front. Judges. Blood. Their wigs making women of them. I said "I have a responsibility." I thought I should show some concern. I leaped up and began pacing on the carpet.

The Provost said "Let me put it this way Stephen. You have a certain responsibility for the undergraduates that come to your house—" I could smash his room up: hit him

183

and get arrested. "—but it is something in your favour that an undergraduate should come to you at all." I paused by a leather chair and looked out on to the graves. There was the smell of roast lamb for lunch. "There is a risk in these friendships of course, that those in authority recognize. But it's not as if he had been drinking at your house". I said quickly "He had been previously." The Provost said "There is a danger in this Stephen of a sort of neurotic self-blame: I hope you don't mind my talking bluntly." I frowned and turned away from the window. My hands were in my pockets; my toe in some pattern of the carpet. The Provost said "There would also be the extremely unfortunate result of any more publicity for his family or the college." My toe moved along a Persian scroll. The Provost watched me. He said "I'm sorry to hear your wife has been ill, Stephen. How is the child getting along?" I said "They say it's going to die."

He was too old for this. A diplomat, bored, deadpan. If you did nothing long enough something happened. He came and stood close to me. He said "Anything I can do." He meant it. I said "Thank you." I wanted to stay here for a while: cool, civilised. Put my feet up. I said "Well there it is." The Provost said "How's the book going?" I said "I'll be losing it soon at Didcot Station." He smiled. We were fitting in again. Two old homosexuals in a jigsaw. He began "When Provost Jones was doing his *Words and Objects*—" I could hardly believe this. I looked round to make sure. The green walls, table-cloth, smell of dried skin and shaving. I finished my sherry. I thought—I might even gain prestige: through murder and adultery.

Outside again in the bright sun. Today I went to the

hospital and they said there was no change. The baby lay on its white gauze waiting for it. Life or death. William with the marks on his face. Anna with her scarf out flying in the wind. The trees were like an army marching. I have always noticed trees. I have forgotten my rose-beds and my garden. There was not much more of summer now. A lot of people in summer, too many for the earth. An ache in my head and stomach. I had a memory. Perhaps if I grew up my memory would die. What had really happened? One thing I must not, cannot believe; that the death of William had to do with the death of my baby. This was superstition. Just the ache, knowledge of it. Something.

The courtroom was a miniature court of law. There were raised pews and boxes like unearthed foundations. I had to say—I suppose he was coming to see me. At the ceiling some plaster work, my long intelligent hair. But now. I had not thought enough about this now. Too frightened, nothing to be done about it. Law is the enemy. Or now there was no enemy. I kept on forgetting this. The old men with blood on their hair. I sat composed, waiting. I thought—I am not going to be able to do this. An earth-quake, terror; the waves breaking. I will stand up and cry— From the dead! From the dead to the dead. They might not listen. They are amiable: you can't beat them.

I was in a pew like a miniature chapel. Questions came out sideways not wanting to be considered. There was a solicitor from William's family, a doctor, the police with papers under their arms. A man whispered "You represent his college?" Everyone whispered. I thought—I no longer know truth nor bravery. A man on a tumbril, watching the face of the crowd. Holding up one of the condemned; a collapsed thing. They drag him out with his feet behind him. Go through the motions.

When it was my turn, my turn, I had been waiting. I stepped up, that quiet thing, so polite, merciful. On a rostrum. I would cry—Citizens! to the millions below. Ordeal by fear. I bowed, put my hands on the ledge. I would do this to the end. "You are—" "Yes." That is what I am. Discreet, two-faced. "And now—" A bunch of papers.

A long way away. I am doing this two years after. Looking back on it. It no longer haunts me. How to describe it then? We are all so much older: my children play in the garden. It happened. What else? The great distance of the sky, the universe. Things are important at the time. Life hangs on them. Then they are over.

"And when you came across the car—". I could answer this. A man with grey hair and spectacles. The car had overturned. One wheel was up the bank. The engine was ticking. "And what was the position of the deceased?" I could answer this. At the bottom, at the left hand side, on the window. "Where he appeared to have fallen?" "Yes." How accurate are words? I am a professional. Paradoxes. He was asking something else. "And what was his condition?" Condition? "He was dead." "How do you know?" How do I know? "I felt him." How inadequate! This was written down. Something was wrong. I said "There was nothing to do but telephone."

I thought—I have been found guilty of something I did not commit. This is commonplace. I wanted to protest. How does one know when one is dead? Standing with my hands on the rail. The coroner was a large bald man in tweeds. There was about to be a miscarriage of justice.

186

The coroner said "Thank you Mr. Jervis."

William's face was hit on the left side. How could it have been hit on the left side?

I stepped down. Passing me was the doctor. A small dark man from the hospital. In the middle of the night he had been called from some bed. Where William had lain: Rosalind and my small dying baby. His name. The time. Was it so early? Charlie had started driving past the landscape. What was the cause: birth, corruption. The doctor was saying something technical. Which meant that the neck was broken. But how? I was thinking aloud. My face was composed, correct. Something had been wrenched by a blow at an angle. So he must have been looking out of the window. But the doctor did not say— He must have been looking out of the window. I had always known, knew, he had been looking out of the window. How else would his neck have been broken? Or Anna unhurt? Or Anna driving? I thought—I will stand up now and cry—.The coroner said "And was this consonant with the effects of the accident?" The doctor said "Yes." My children and my children's children. On the lawn, among the beech trees. I thought—I will get up and leave. "And what would have caused this blow?" Perhaps the roof as the car turned over. Or some such. He was in a hurry. The doctor. To get to his afternoon off. Golf. The law. That old facade. Thank God for it. What civilisation rests on.

Now what had happened? Now I could think about this. Thank God, you are so kind to me! I am free now: only guilty. I had reached down to William on his left side. I had propped myself with one hand on the windscreen. I had stepped in with one foot, I think, having

187

kicked the door back with a scrunch of metal. I had felt his hand and his temples. I had looked up the empty road with the trees overhead marching. Anna had been staying with me perhaps because I had been having an affair with her. She had come down with me and had sat there on the bank. How difficult it was to remember. I had always cared for Anna. So I had walked up the empty road a lone and heroic figure. And had breathed upon his mouth. Giving life to her. When the police and the ambulance had come I had been standing beneath the stars like the last post above crosses. The good earth, the ploughland and hedgerow. A man in a mackintosh had lifted William by his shoulders and knees. The undertakers were a well-paid job from father to son; took care of everything. I had looked up the road after the ambulance and had said—I am finished. I was always good at acting things. A policeman had asked if he could have just a word with me. I had said—Certainly. We had walked up to the house. William had been on his own. Anna was in the house. I would look after the small crowd by the graveside; the emotions, handkerchiefs. Anna had been driving. My friend Charlie would be involved: he was running around after younger women. We would all be disgraced. Anna was not in the drawing room.

People in the courtroom were moving about, packing. The morning hot. The thing was over. The coroner had not said anything.

Anna would be at home now in her own country beside the lake, the fir trees.

It was true it was difficult to remember. What mercy! My children and my children's children. Clarissa with her face like pearls: Alexander beautiful as a poet. Justice and mercy make equal demands on you. Are incompatible. Perhaps I may die now. There are walls behind my eyes. Which way should I have chosen?

I was going back to the college for the last meeting of term. Everything was cleared up now and accepted. There was that old doorway, gate, which I had passed through before. Gate within a gate, narrow, to the porter's lodge. An entrance to those green lawns, gold stone, an organ playing. I stopped the car opposite it and watched. I put my hand to my forehead. There was no scar. Perhaps I would soon get used to it. Mankind has so little control; just puts one foot in front of the other. Slow; excitable. If someone were to ask me—a sudden rush of howls up the street, talons, the faces of bats. I got out of the car and walked towards the porter's lodge. If someone were to ask me, I wouldn't know. I arranged my coat to flow along the pavements, along the walls and up the face of crumbling buildings. I had nearly achieved it. Death. I would say to the porter— Any message? He would look on a notice board on a glass-box, his voice coming sideways, not wanting consideration. The man in the courtroom asking questions. The porter gave me a piece of paper, folded, with my name on it. I thanked him. I went on into the courtyard with my eye-brows raised and the two tortured furrows in my forehead. People passed me with hushed voices. Something had happened. I did not open the piece of paper. I crossed the lawn, the gravel, looking up and down between stone pinnacles. I bared my teeth. An eccentric. A late vision of hell. There was a bell going somewhere. I thought—Anna with her head on the pillow, having dropped her after I had carried her up the road. But I had not carried her up the road. We all lived for protection. I went on through gothic arches, cloisters, monks. Prayer had its efficacy. Anna had gone up to the room alone, slept alone, woken up alone. We had not much helped her. I began to open the message on the piece of paper. In the committee room there would be the other fellows of the college, my colleagues, on leather chairs. A molecule of disease or energy. I opened the paper and read—*Mr. Jervis, your wife telephoned to say that the child is much better and will be all right.* I thought—Well that is something. I was on some stone steps like Faust. I thought—How odd things are, their timing. I opened the door to the committee room and I saw them all there— Tommy Parker in his corduroy jacket, Arthurson dry as bacon, Hedge the mathematician with his small steel spectacles. They had not expected me. I nodded. The Provost said "Stephen! Shall we begin now?" I sat down. We had these meetings once a fortnight to discuss college business. We achieved there a communal mind, a sort of séance. I sat down and became one of them, my mind a wall, going out at right angles to me. The meeting began. The Provost made a speech. He had his arms in a V on the table. All of us would be dug up here in another six hundred years. Or would remain permanently in a fresco. I had wanted some sort of destruction out of boredom with my work, my personality. William had died. We were all now waiting. Men lounging, distrustful, showing off round the table. I was still holding the message from Rosalind. I would go to the hospital. I would run there. I would howl through the streets and say—.I raised my hand again to my forehead. I did not feel anything. Someone was talking of endowments, trusts, percentages. This was a hot summer. I would run to the hospital past the ashes, the lava, the skeletons with their knees drawn up. I would say—I am alive! At least I had done something: had risked, taken a chance on it. There were cries from the grass and the people running. My child was going to be all right! Through the window of the committee room, the leaves of the trees waved: there were edges of buildings moulded, carved against the sky. I felt myself still in a cage of narrow walls. I could say—I am feeling I have got to go now. This was what I was so often thinking. I would say—My child is all right! Get up and go back along those grey stone passages, walk to freedom. Black stuff, clothes, dust; round the room these things I was so frightened of. Eyeholes, devils. Through them that by which we had all been possessed; the dark thing, fear. The devils sat outside the rabbit holes gave us a stroke on the neck. Like quicksilver. I could not do this any more. I could move: run. To what? I was old enough now. Nothing. I thought—I am going to go to the hospital. There I will meet my child, who is alive. What joy! I began to arrange my papers. To the sun, to the silver sand and palm trees. What a marvel life was! The small thing sleeping with its breath, its heartbeat. How we loved, would love it! All of the past in its head, its heart. The air coming in.

I thought—So it does not matter much now. The earth had changed. I was sorry, but how could you have life without this ache, this terror. How could you have joy? We were sitting round the table like masks, nothing behind us. Outside the world was roaring: huge cranes above a ruined car. William; Anna. But what could I do? I loved William, and Anna. When I was first in love with Rosalind I ran through streets in the dark adoring, adoring her. She floated in a white nightdress out of windows. There was death: there was so much beauty. The small thing with its breath coming easier. The broken glass; the flywheel.

I was becoming too happy again. I was behind a table, thinking, having been through a certain fear. The brain had a speck of acid in it. Outside it was a bright windy day. I had walked this way a few minutes ago. My child was alive. I have not really explained this. We write in order to grasp it; to make a grab at the air. I wanted to say something about the world; about the meaning of it. Actions have not much to do with this. It is more a feeling: this is what life is. I thought I would go to Rosalind and say—I told you so: there is magic in my fingers. The dead thing carried from the car. The live thing in its oxygen tent. There are huge migrations of birds, of spirits. Winter and black clouds. The man surviving. I would run up the steps of the hospital to my angels and I would say—This is where William lay: This my child. Always two parts of me. I was one of the people round the table in the committee room: I was running up the steps of the hospital to greet Rosalind. From where I am writing now I can see my children playing. There are three of them, by a rose-bed, a line of fir trees. Shall I say—There was that time, a year or two ago, when Rosalind was pregnant. We were all so much younger then. We have forgotten some of it. Some of it has been changed. I have not seen Anna again. I do not see much of Charlie now. One of us may be sitting round the table in the committee room; one of us may be playing with the child that is alive. Charlie is the writer: he will write this book. But I wanted to say—This is the point of it. Remember it happy; the sun in your eyes.

An Afterword

The novels of Nicholas Mosley grow from a great desire for order; also, from a recognition that order is impossible. The point, as *Accident* demonstrates, is not to despair over this crux but to act and thus to find its meaning.

By the term *accident* Mosley signifies both the constituting event of this novel—William's fatal car crash—and a specific definition in philosophical discourse: the accidental is that which participates neither in substance nor in essence, and which therefore obeys none of the causal rules of substantial being. It is purely fortuitous, not in the modern sense of probabilistic chance but in the oldest (Hellenic) sense: during "an accident" events "just happen." In ethical philosophy the idea is also linked to Indeterminism, the theory that events sometimes unfold absolutely without cause.

But novels are "plotted." And it is of the essence of this novel, Mosley's sixth, that its elegantly plotted sequence be read as a play on the romantic thriller. In other words, it is a plot of detection. Narrating two years after the facts, Stephen Jervis opens with the fatal event (accident or crime?; or is the only crime Stephen's suppression of evidence?), then he puts dead-center in his story a long analepsis whose point (as in any detective plot) must be to "explain" causes and thus to "solve" enigmas. Last, Stephen closes by telling, like any good detective, his actions following upon that knowledge of causes. Ironically, however, the middle chapters solve no mysteries about the accident; still more, in the end Stephen acts *by not acting.* Having "read" from crash evidence that Anna von Graz was driving, without a license, and after drinking, and that William died while riding with his head stuck absurdly out the side window; aware furthermore that he is legally responsible to report these things—knowing all of this, Stephen acts by keeping quiet about them through the inquest. His silent inaction at the finish thus balances his action at the start of his narrative, when he not only leapt to Anna's aid but also told police an untrue "story" about the accident.

What has happened to Stephen between these antipodes? For one, his wife, Rosalind, has given premature birth. That is Mosley's subplot. The main plot has to do with the conditions necessary for the story itself to be told. And its carefully ordered plot emerges from a stylistic practice which tends, beautifully and paradoxically, towards fracture and dislocation. His is a way of "leaving out connecting sentences," a continual "leap-frog of the mind," as with the stories which his colleagues tell over lunch. One does well to consider the analogy there. Just as the infant survives by overcoming the deadly, fortuitous circumstances of its birth, so the narrative grows by surmounting accidental gaps which would be fatal to ordinary narrative, especially a detective plot. Every nuance of style—from the fragmentary sentences to the disorienting shifts of episodes or chapters—mitigates against the well-ordered end.

Mosley's end, while not the well-tuned stuff of a romantic thriller *is* ordered around perfectly ordinary needs. The marriages and jobs endure; the bureaucracies put their officious, wrongheaded imprimatur on accidental events. "We know all this," as Stephen so often says. What we scarcely know and must learn, with him, is the linguistic nature of that everyday reality.

In this Mosley shares the concerns of contemporaries on both sides of the Atlantic—of writers like Iris Murdoch and John Hawkes, Gilbert Sorrentino and J. G. Ballard. Mosley too is suspicious of received knowledge in all its effects on everyday experience. Still more significantly he is suspicious of how our everyday experiences are rationalized, plotted, from the moment they slide away from us. Stephen claims: "You live in the present, which does not exist; it exists in memory." And *Accident* argues that what is "real" is *not* a text—for it is essentially non-narrative, accidental. But Mosley adds the proviso that as "reality" becomes past it is accessible *only* as a "text"—when it is known through episodic memory, in story-telling.

In his preface to *Catastrophe Practice*, a 1979 collection of plays and fictions, Mosley would recall Bertold Brecht's admonition that a drama "should be a demonstration." Not a "representation" of rarefied, whole characters and events, a play instead should demonstrate the very complexities involved in observing anything. Brecht's example, as Mosley notes, involved an eyewitness at "a street-accident" explaining "to bystanders what has taken place." Inevitably the explanation involves his own categories of feeling and knowledge, which themselves become objects of scrutiny. Something like this has been going on in the novels of Nicholas Mosley ever since his breakthrough work in *Accident* (1966) and *Impossible Object* (1968), books which successfully left traditional representation behind. For example, the idea of "believable," whole characters disappears into the complexity of Stephen's observation that we are several, perhaps many performing selves during the course of a day. Charlie similarly observes: "We know too much about characters and actions." Indeed, as for the idea of narrative causality, it fades when the heart of Stephen's story (the pre-accident months) fails to disclose anything about the accident which one might not have induced in the first place from a careful reading of the "clues" in chapter 1.

Instead of solving these readerly puzzles, *Accident* engages the question of the truth-status of "fictions," and therefore of the truth-status of what we claim was "reality." Consider for instance the problem of who is supposed to have written the text we have just finished reading. Is it Charlie, the novelist, or Stephen, who looks remarkably like Charlie? The narrator claims, in his last paragraph, that "Charlie is the writer: he will write this book"; there is no "realistic" detail in the story to resolve that puzzle. Add to this the way other characters resemble each other in appearance: Anna and Laura for example. Or characters resemble each other in action: Charlie once stuck *his* head out the window of a moving automobile, too, and suffered a (minor) accident. Still more troubling is Stephen's suggestion that *he* was in the fatal car: "I had been all night at a party. I had driven off with a girl in a car. I had crashed." Such enigmatic resemblances and coincidences keep adding up. And the sum of it all must be our understanding that literary fictions can never "imitate" or "represent" experience, which does not behave in so orderly a manner. Literary fictions always only imitate the "languages" by which we give formal shape to experience.

Now language, as the French theorists have instructed us, is both *langue* and *parole*, a system and a practice, the desire for orderly grammars and the frustration of accidents. And it follows that ethics, created through the medium of language, must be subject to the same antinomies.

The genius of *Accident* lies in its humanistic "demonstration" that the best way to work through these paradoxes is by learning to manipulate them. Such is the problem thrust upon Stephen Jervis "by accident." The reviewers almost all noted how he is a masterful tactician with words, though to them it was mainly a trait—perhaps rather selfish—of "character." See his tactics, instead, as a disclosure of the complexities in narrative discourse. The boating scene, or "impression," in chapter 12 is brilliant proof of what he can do in the Great Tradition of novelistic art. (One may also read it as Mosley's farewell to techniques he mastered in his first five novels.) He can as easily "do" anecdotal, philosophical, practical, legal, comical, or theological modes of discourse. Such an interplay demonstrates that one's ability to construct and manipulate hypothetical, alternative structures—the worlds of stories for instance—is a condition of social existence. In miniature, the Oxford dons' stories about "Provost Jones" are proof of just that much. To Mosley, however, there must be more.

The great modernist novels—Ford's *The Good Soldier* or Faulkner's *The Sound and the Fury*—always resolve conflicts in discourse by recontextualizing them at some higher level of authority. Postmodern writers make no such move. Their resolution is through an awareness of the linguistic bases of knowledge. That awareness brings with it a suspicion of words like "realism" because, as Mosley well knows, we have too easily used them to connote our sense of continuity, connection, and causality—then awarded privileged status to that sense. To his American counterparts, like John Hawkes and Thomas Pynchon, that awareness often also means dark comedy and apocalypse.

There must be more. The interplay of language confers the

freedom of choice, and, with it, responsibility. Such was Stephen's argument to Anna von Graz at their earliest tutorials. Having lived that argument through, Stephen concludes, not in the darkness of absurdity or despair, but once more a father in the midst of playing children. "This is the point of it," he writes. "Remember it happy; the sun in your eyes."

STEVEN WEISENBERGER
University of Kentucky

DALKEY ARCHIVE PAPERBACKS

FICTION

BARNES, DJUNA. *Ladies Almanack*	9.95
BARNES, DJUNA. *Ryder*	9.95
CHARTERIS, HUGO. *The Tide Is Right*	9.95
CRAWFORD, STANLEY. *Some Instructions to My Wife*	7.95
CUSACK, RALPH. *Cadenza*	7.95
DOWELL, COLEMAN. *Too Much Flesh and Jabez*	8.00
ERNAUX, ANNIE. *Cleaned Out*	9.95
FIRBANK, RONALD. *Complete Short Stories*	9.95
GASS, WILLIAM H. *Willie Masters' Lonesome Wife*	7.95
GRAINVILLE, PATRICK. *The Cave of Heaven*	10.95
MacLOCHLAINN, ALF. *Out of Focus*	5.95
MARKSON, DAVID. *Springer's Progress*	9.95
MARKSON, DAVID. *Wittgenstein's Mistress*	9.95
MOSLEY, NICHOLAS. *Accident*	9.95
MOSLEY, NICHOLAS. *Impossible Object*	7.95
MOSLEY, NICHOLAS. *Judith*	10.95
QUENEAU, RAYMOND. *The Last Days*	9.95
QUENEAU, RAYMOND. *Pierrot Mon Ami*	7.95
ROUBAUD, JACQUES. *The Great Fire of London*	12.95
SEESE, JUNE AKERS. *What Waiting Really Means*	7.95
SORRENTINO, GILBERT. *Imaginative Qualities of Actual Things*	9.95
SORRENTINO, GILBERT. *Splendide-Hôtel*	5.95
SORRENTINO, GILBERT. *Steelwork*	9.95
STEPHENS, MICHAEL. *Season at Coole*	7.95
TUSQUETS, ESTHER. *Stranded*	9.95
VALENZUELA, LUISA. *He Who Searches*	8.00
WOOLF, DOUGLAS. *Wall to Wall*	7.95
ZUKOFSKY, LOUIS. *Collected Fiction*	9.95

NONFICTION

MATHEWS, HARRY. *20 Lines a Day*	8.95
ROUDIEZ, LEON S. *French Fiction Revisited*	14.95
SHKLOVSKY, VIKTOR. *Theory of Prose*	14.95

POETRY

ALFAU, FELIPE. *Sentimental Songs (La poesia cursi)*	9.95
ANSEN, ALAN. *Contact Highs: Selected Poems*	11.95
FAIRBANKS, LAUREN. *Muzzle Thyself*	9.95

For a complete catalog of our titles, or to order any of these books, write to Dalkey Archive Press, 1817 N. 79th Ave., Elmwood Park, IL 60635. One book, 10% off; two books or more, 20% off; add $3.00 postage and handling.